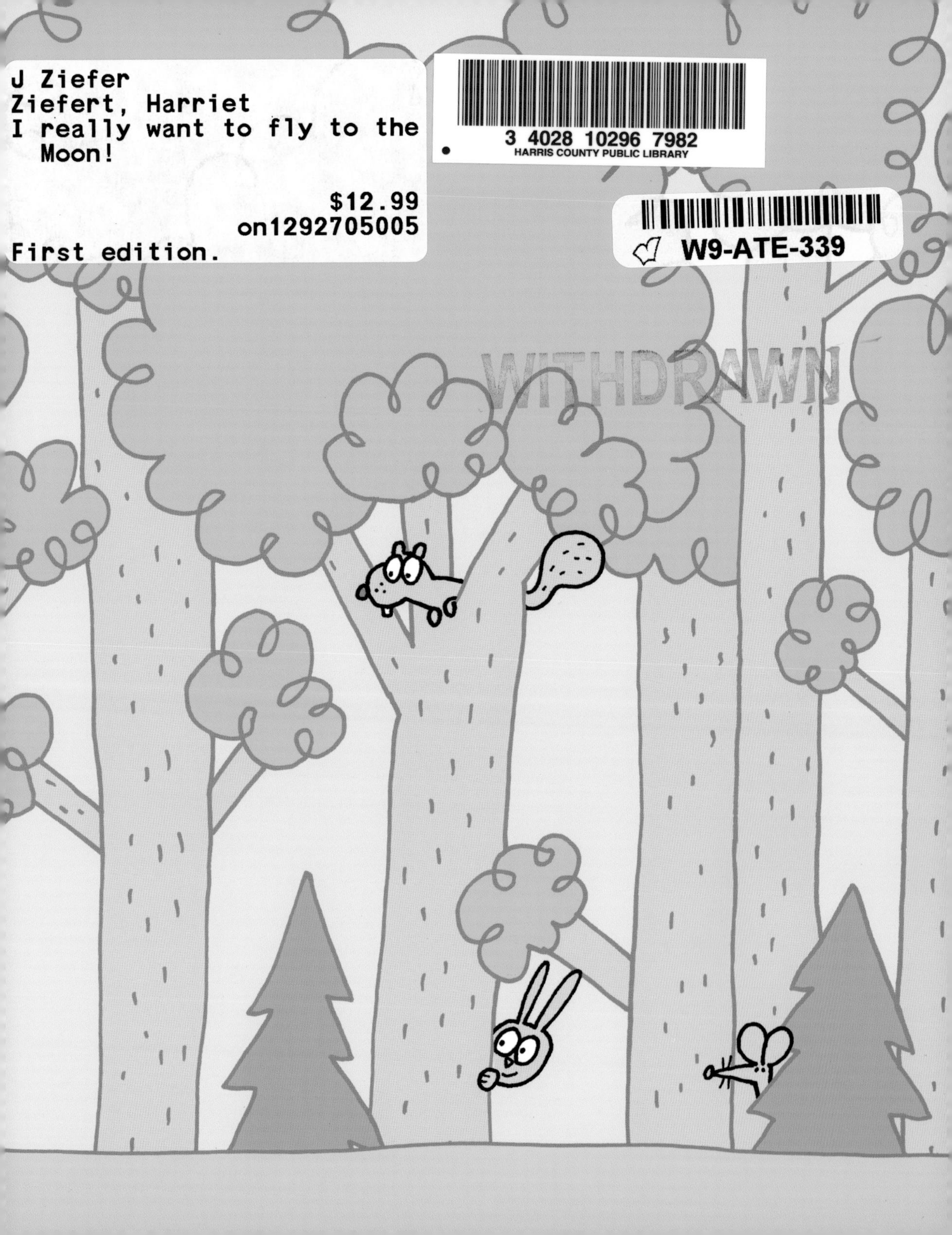

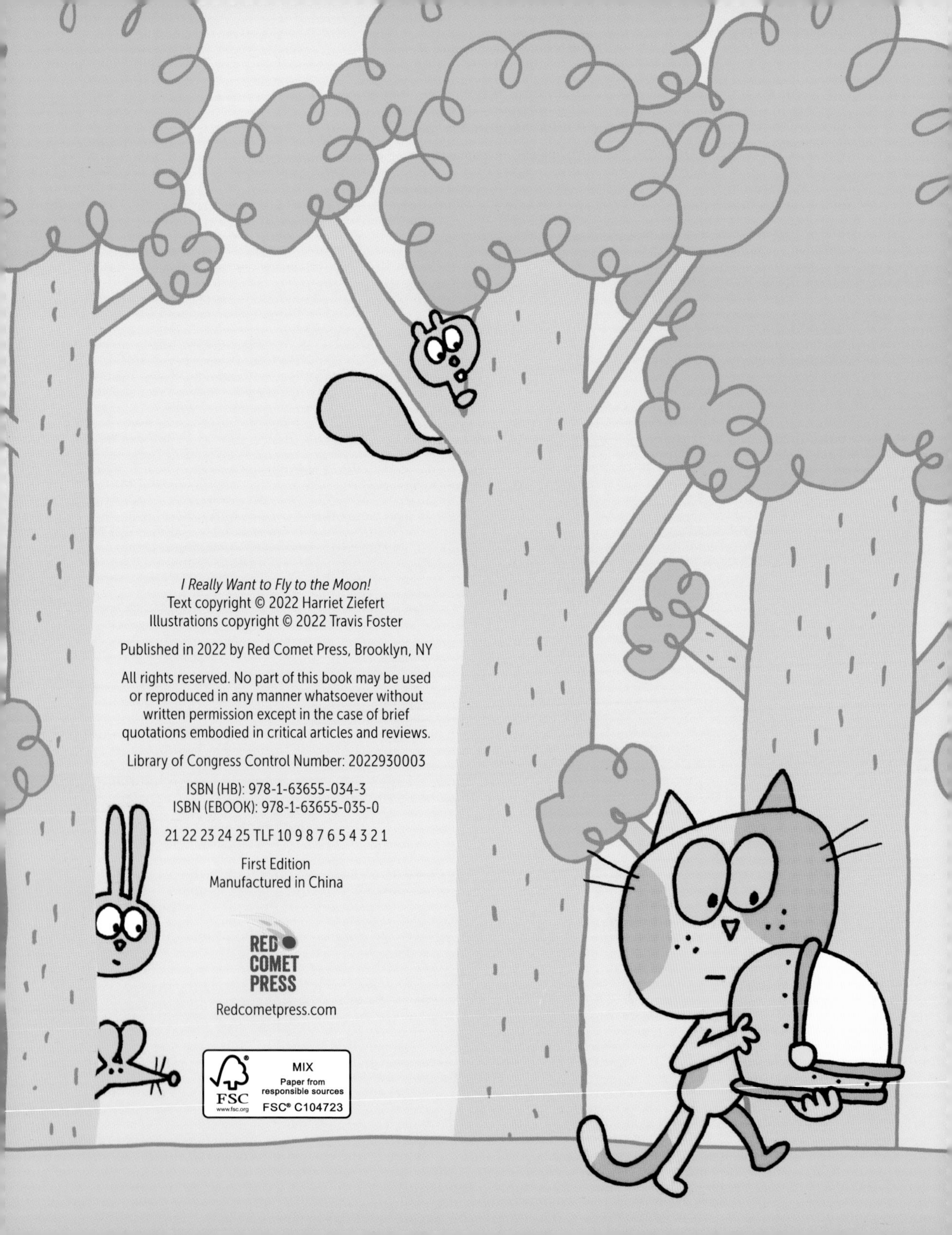

I Really Want to Fly to the Moon!

Published in 2022 by Red Comet Press, Brooklyn, NY

Library of Congress Control Number: 2022930003

ISBN (HB): 978-1-63655-034-3
ISBN (EBOOK): 978-1-63655-035-0

21 22 23 24 25 TLF 10 9 8 7 6 5 4 3 2 1

First Edition
Manufactured in China

RED COMET PRESS

Redcometpress.com

MIX
Paper from responsible sources
FSC® C104723

A REALLY BIRD STORY

Harriet Ziefert
Illustrations By Travis Foster

I Really Want to Fly to the Moon!

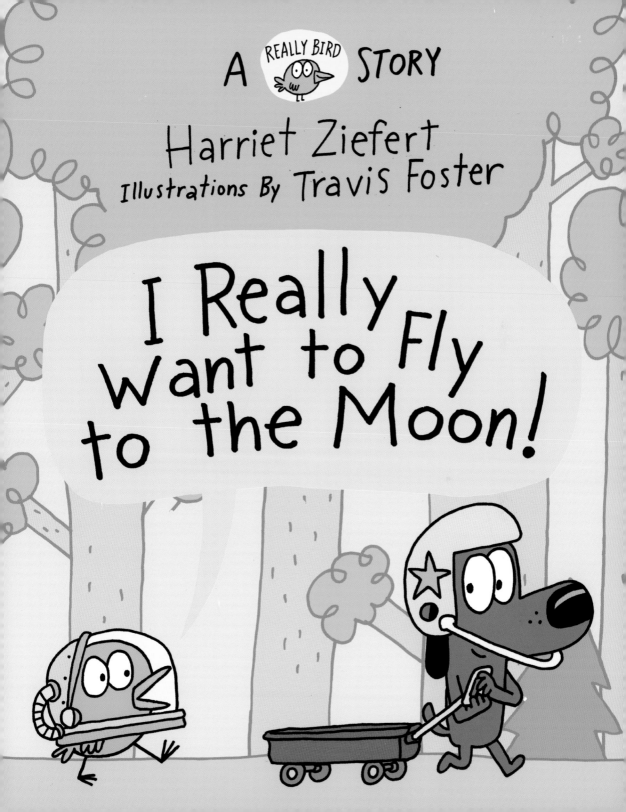

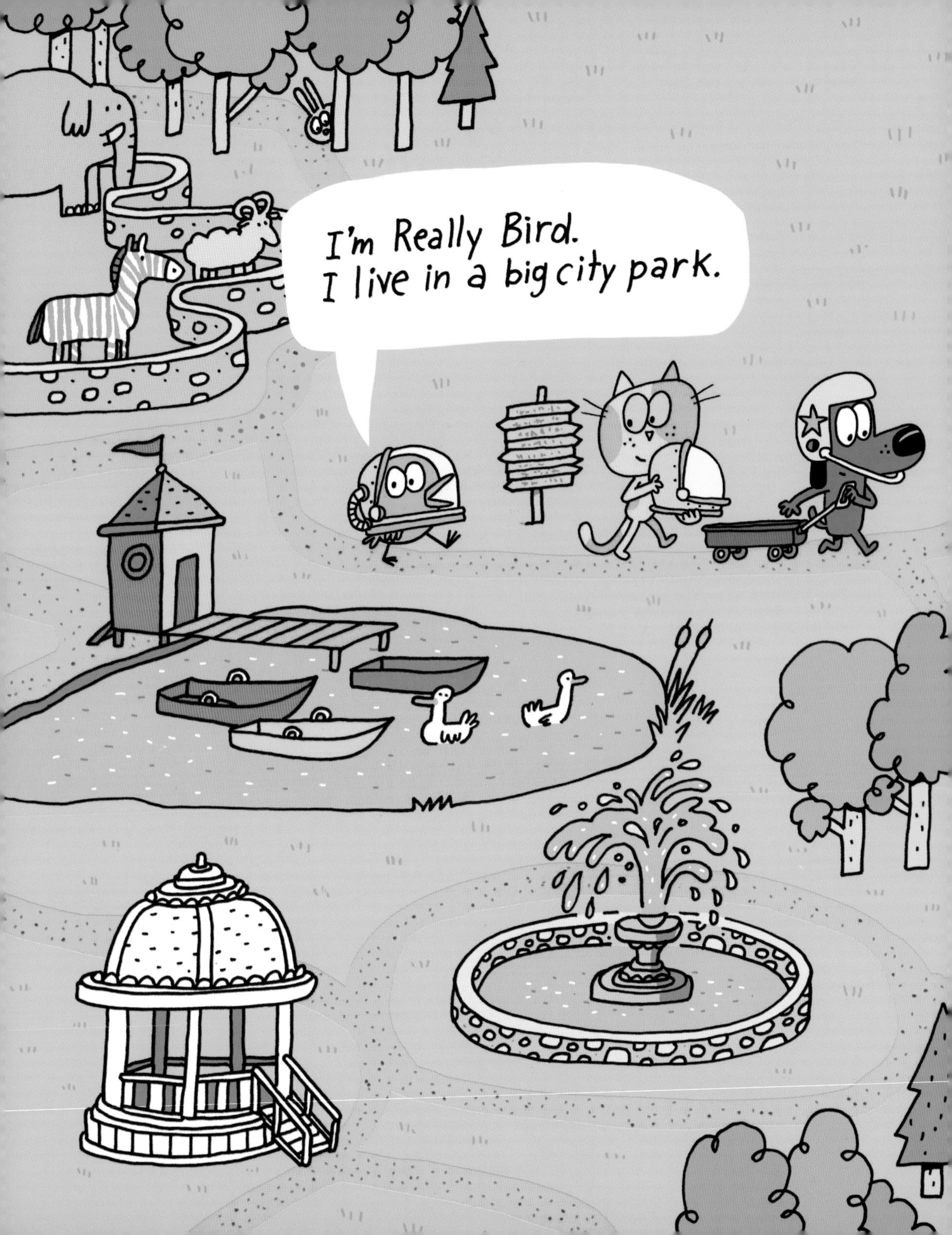
I'm Really Bird.
I live in a big city park.

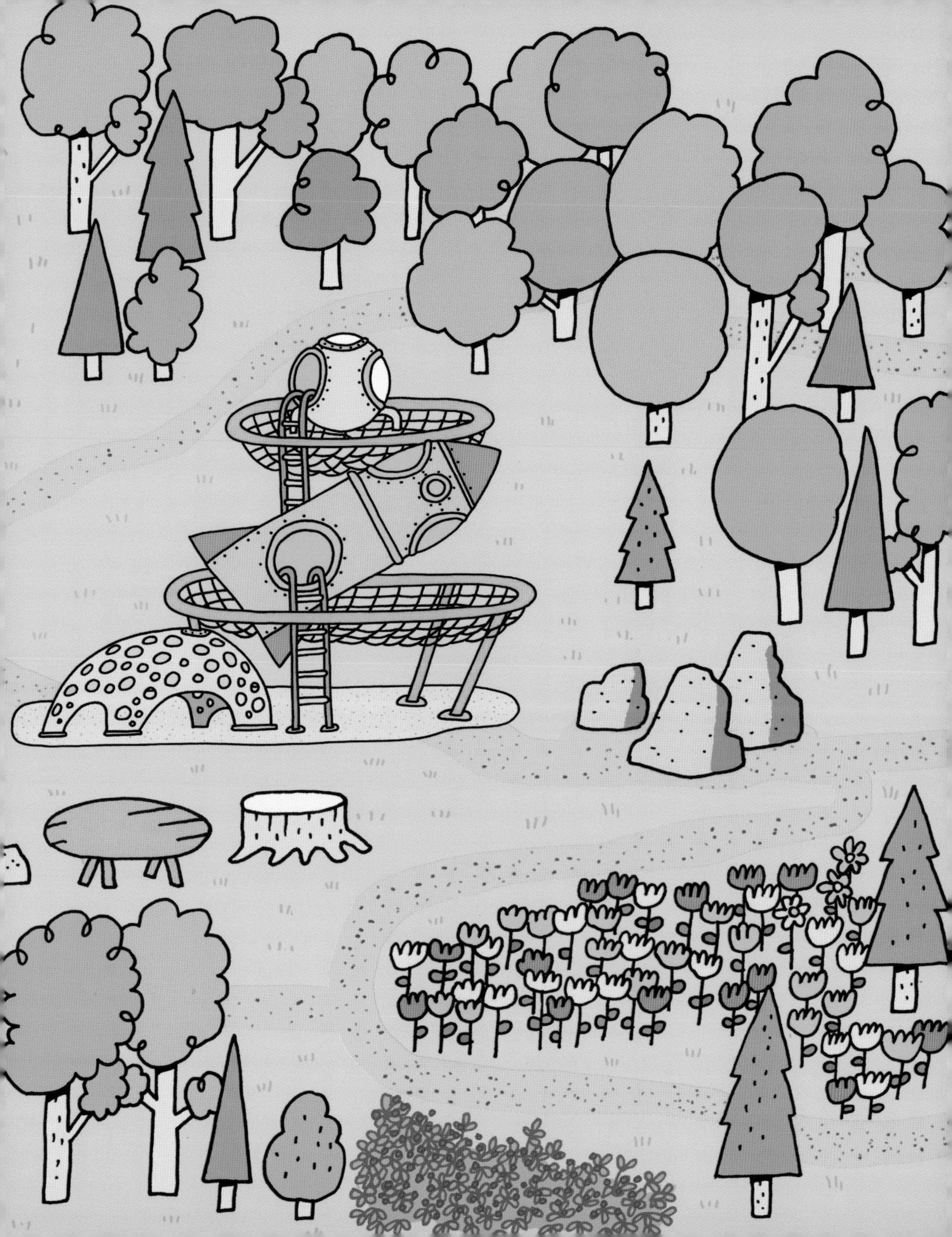

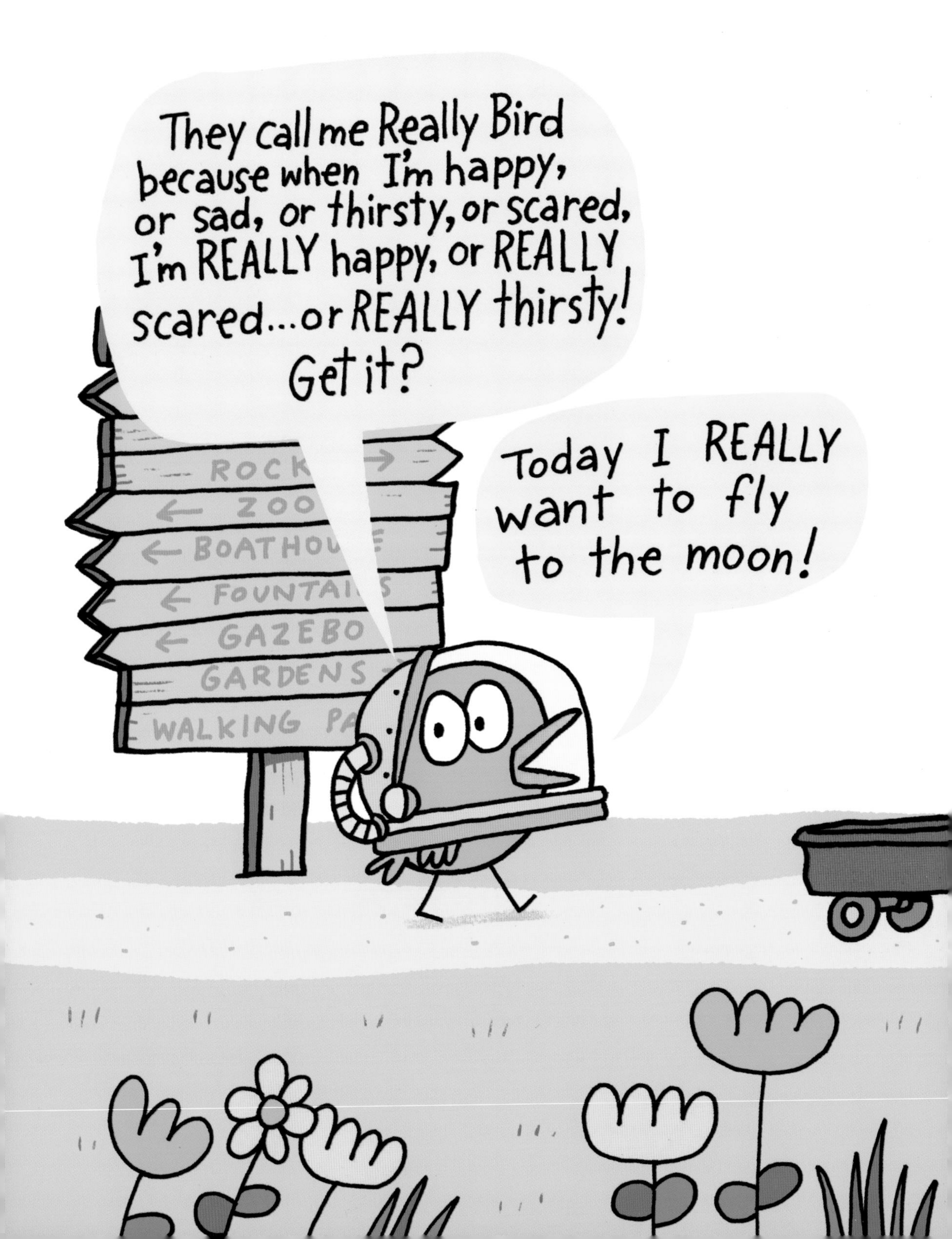
They call me Really Bird because when I'm happy, or sad, or thirsty, or scared, I'm REALLY happy, or REALLY scared...or REALLY thirsty! Get it?
ROCK
ZOO
BOATHOU
FOUNTAI
GAZEBO
GARDENS
WALKING PA
Today I REALLY want to fly to the moon!

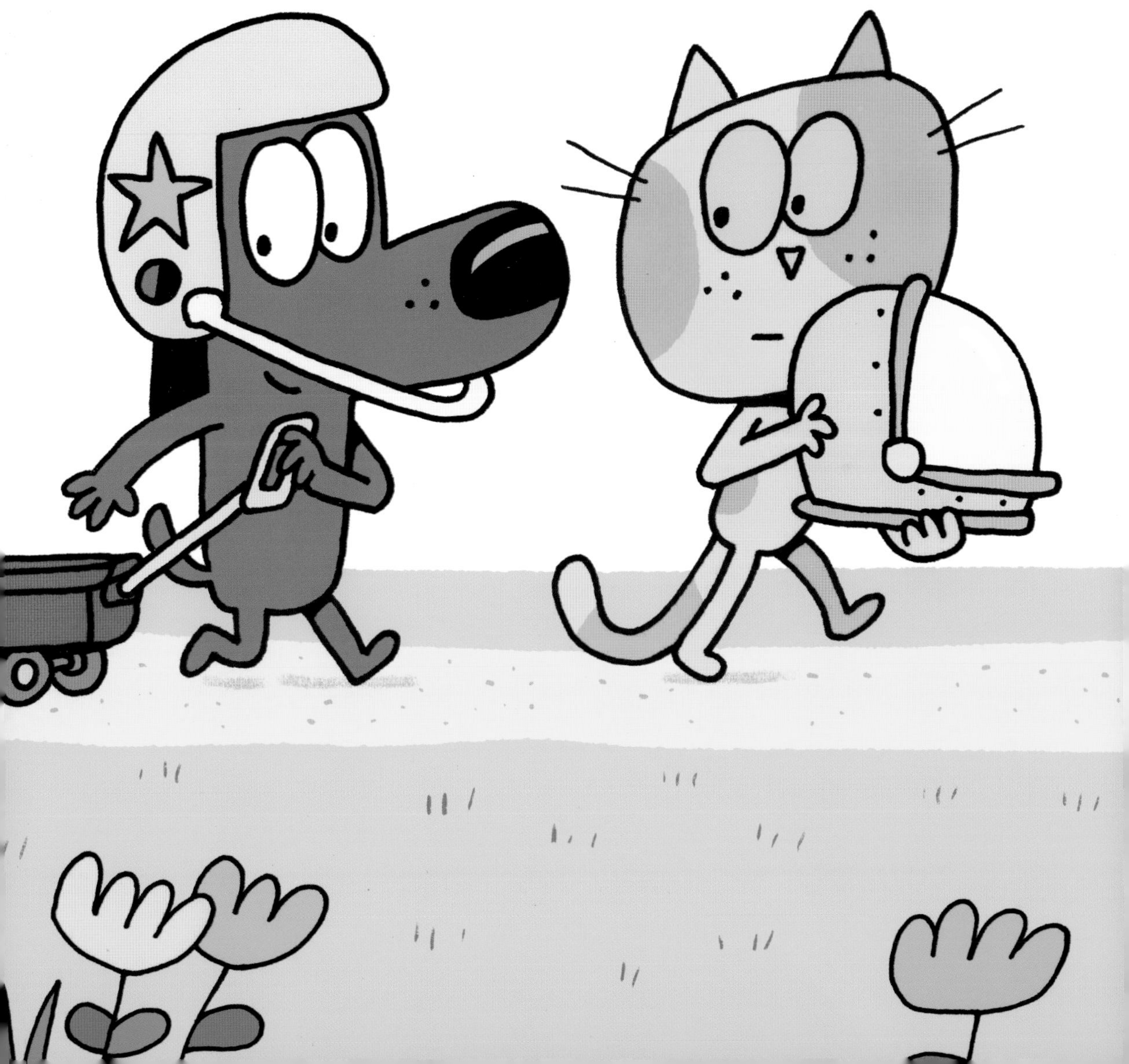

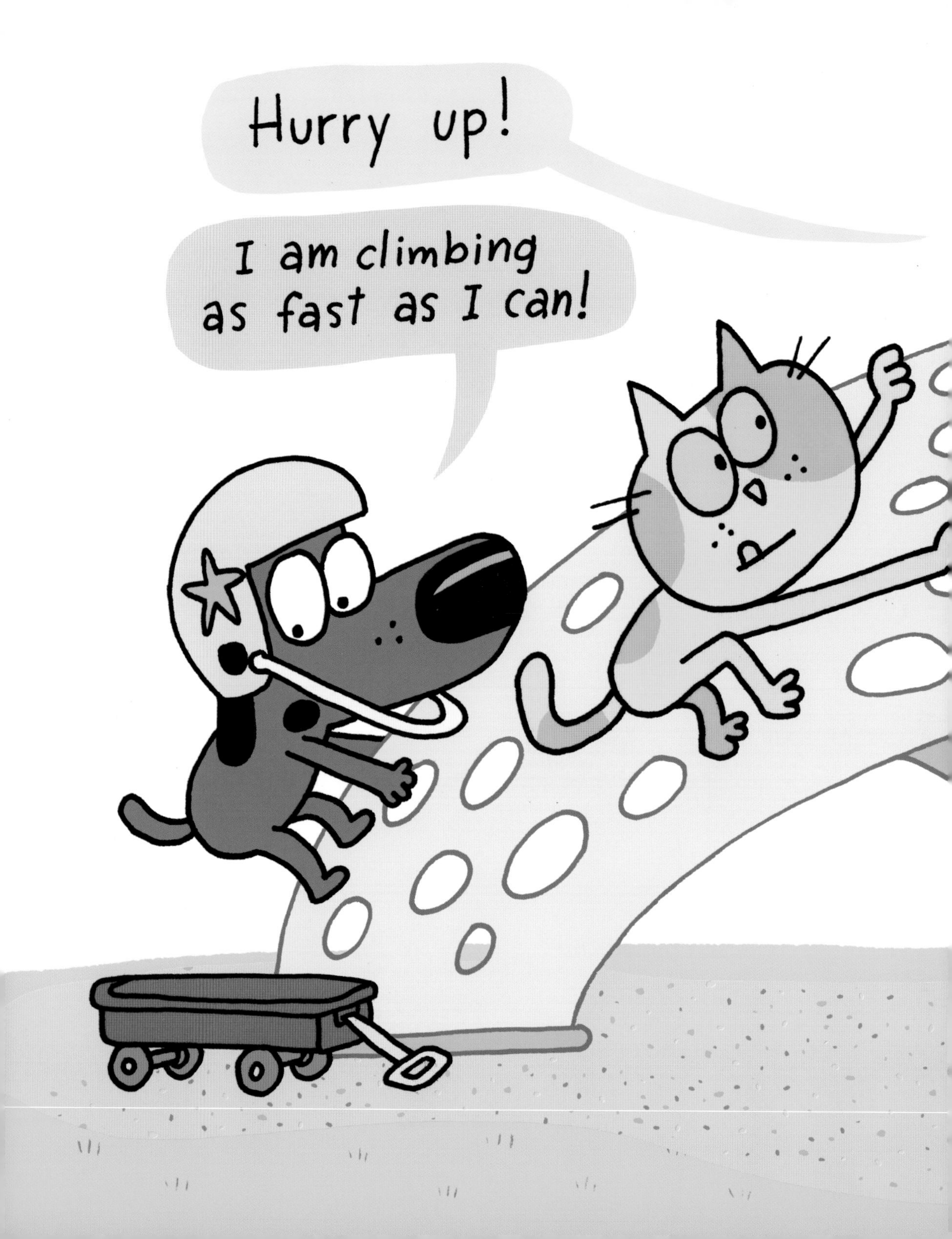
Hurry up!
I am climbing as fast as I can!

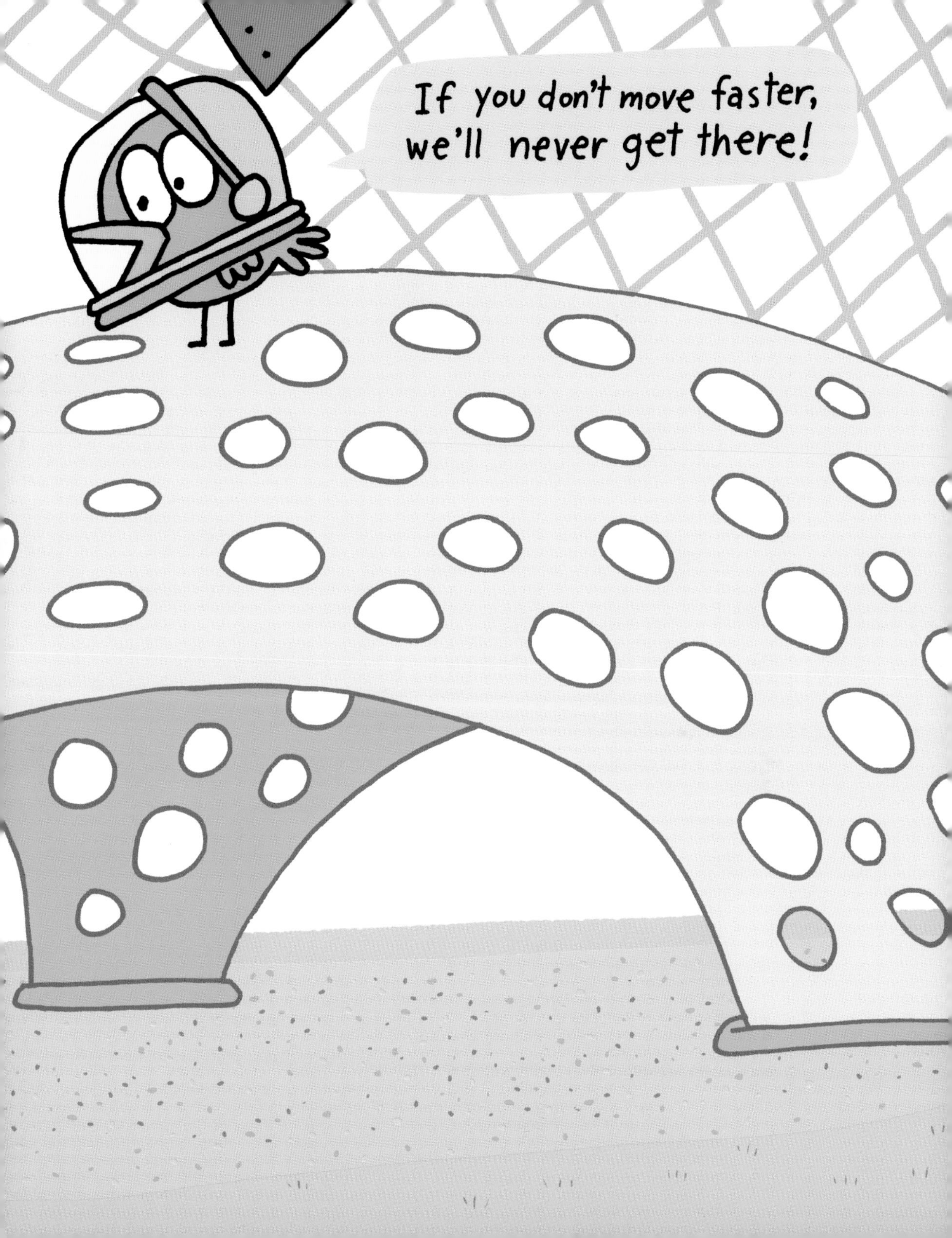
If you don't move faster, we'll never get there!

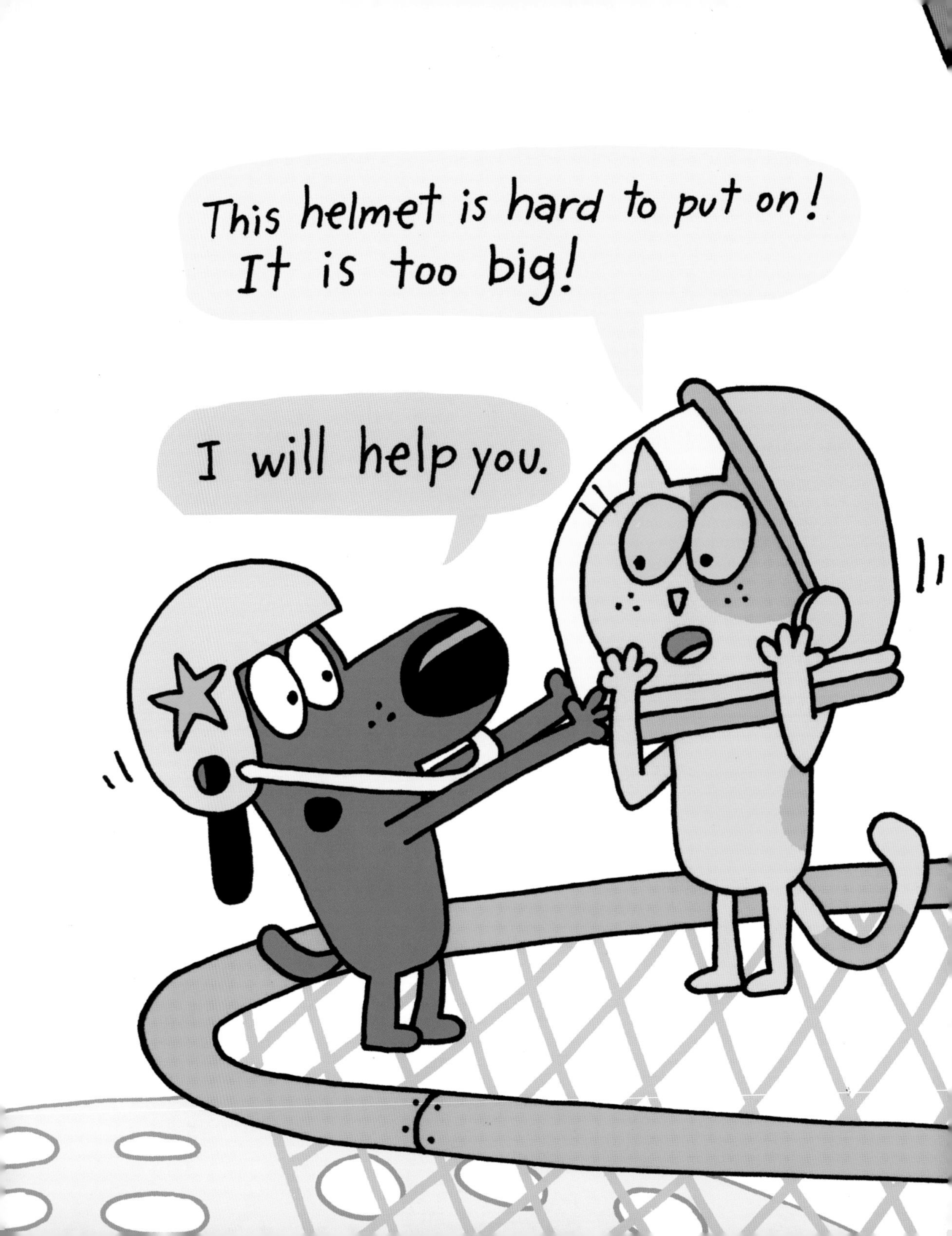
This helmet is hard to put on! It is too big!
I will help you.

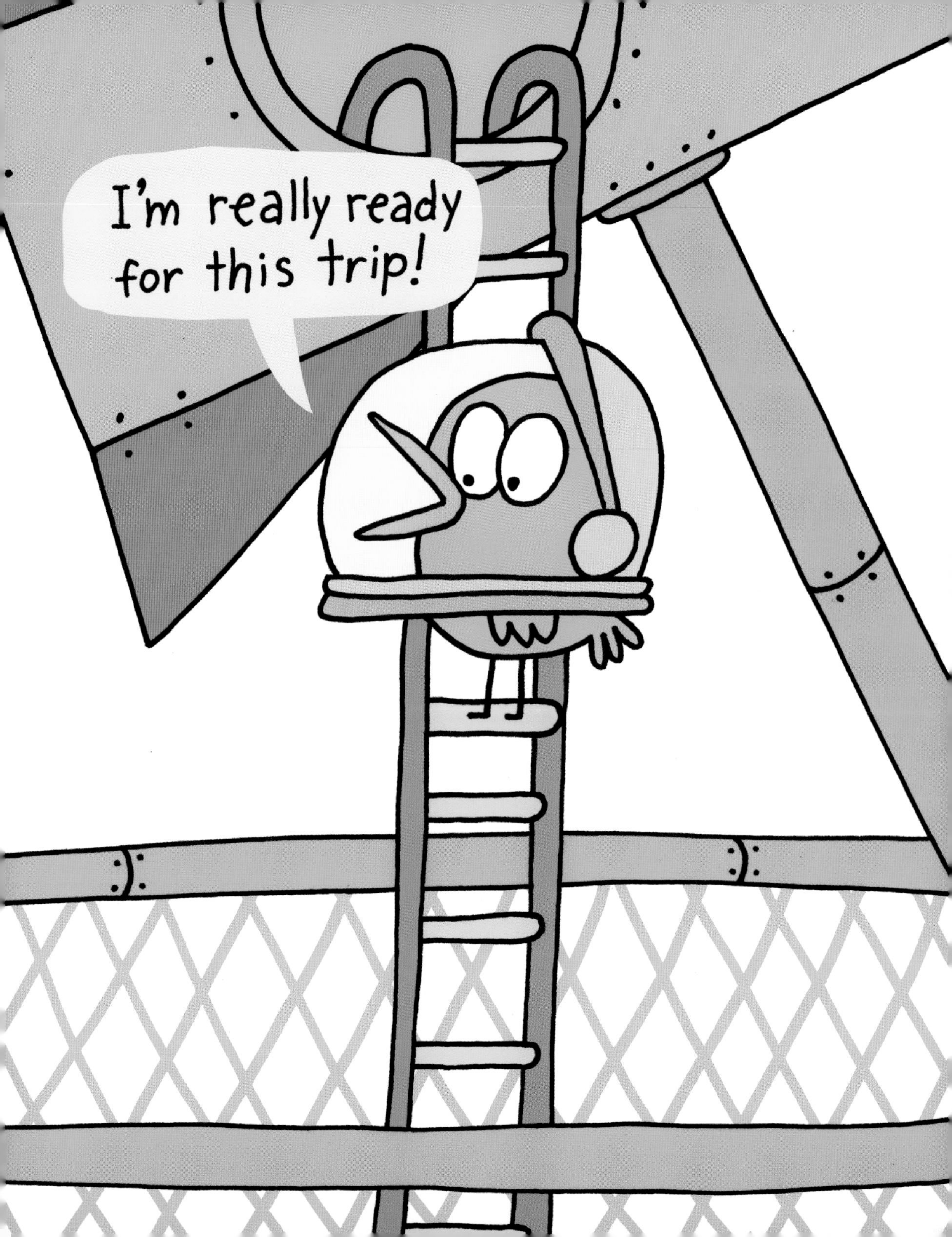
I'm really ready for this trip!

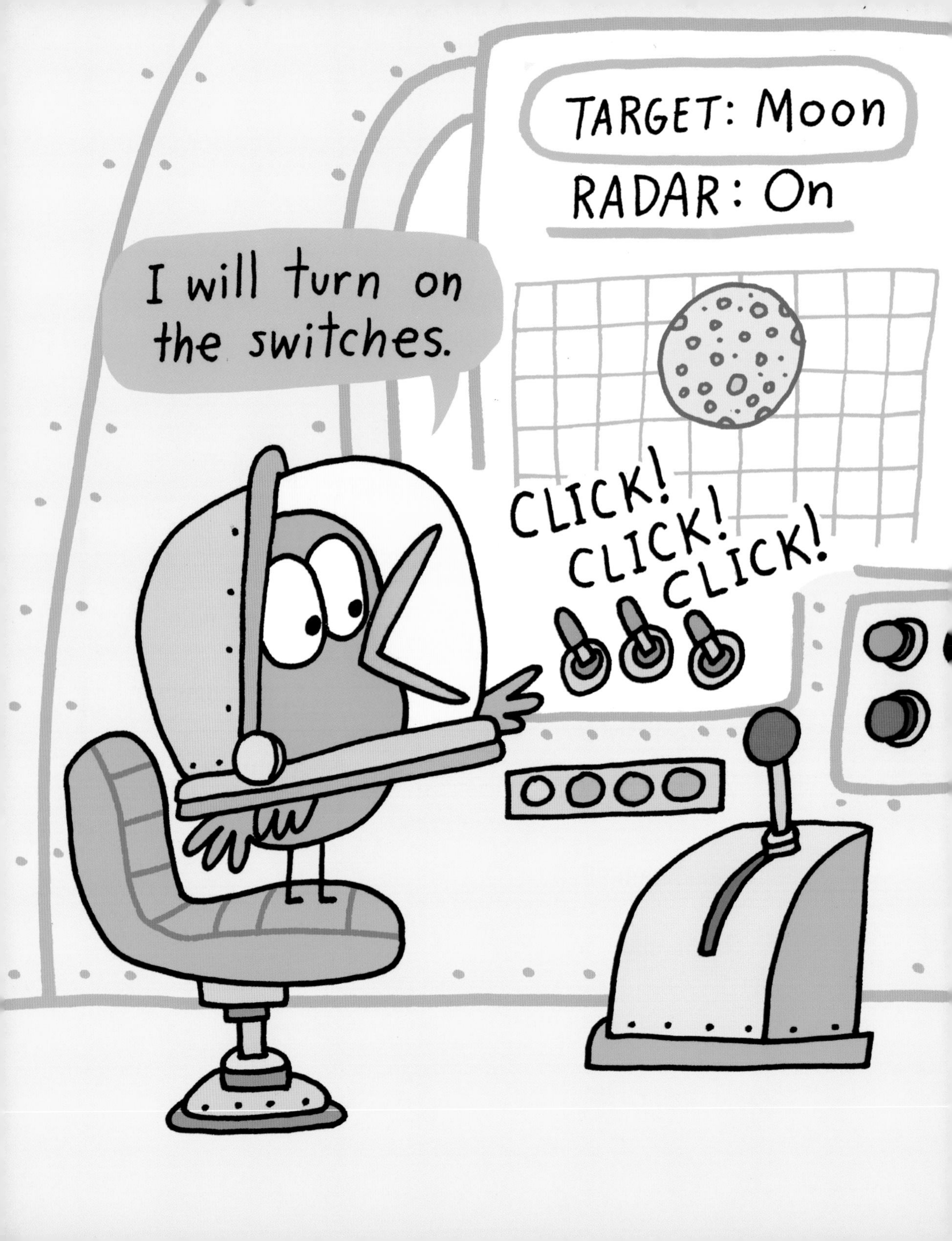
TARGET: Moon
RADAR: On
I will turn on the switches.
CLICK!
CLICK!
CLICK!

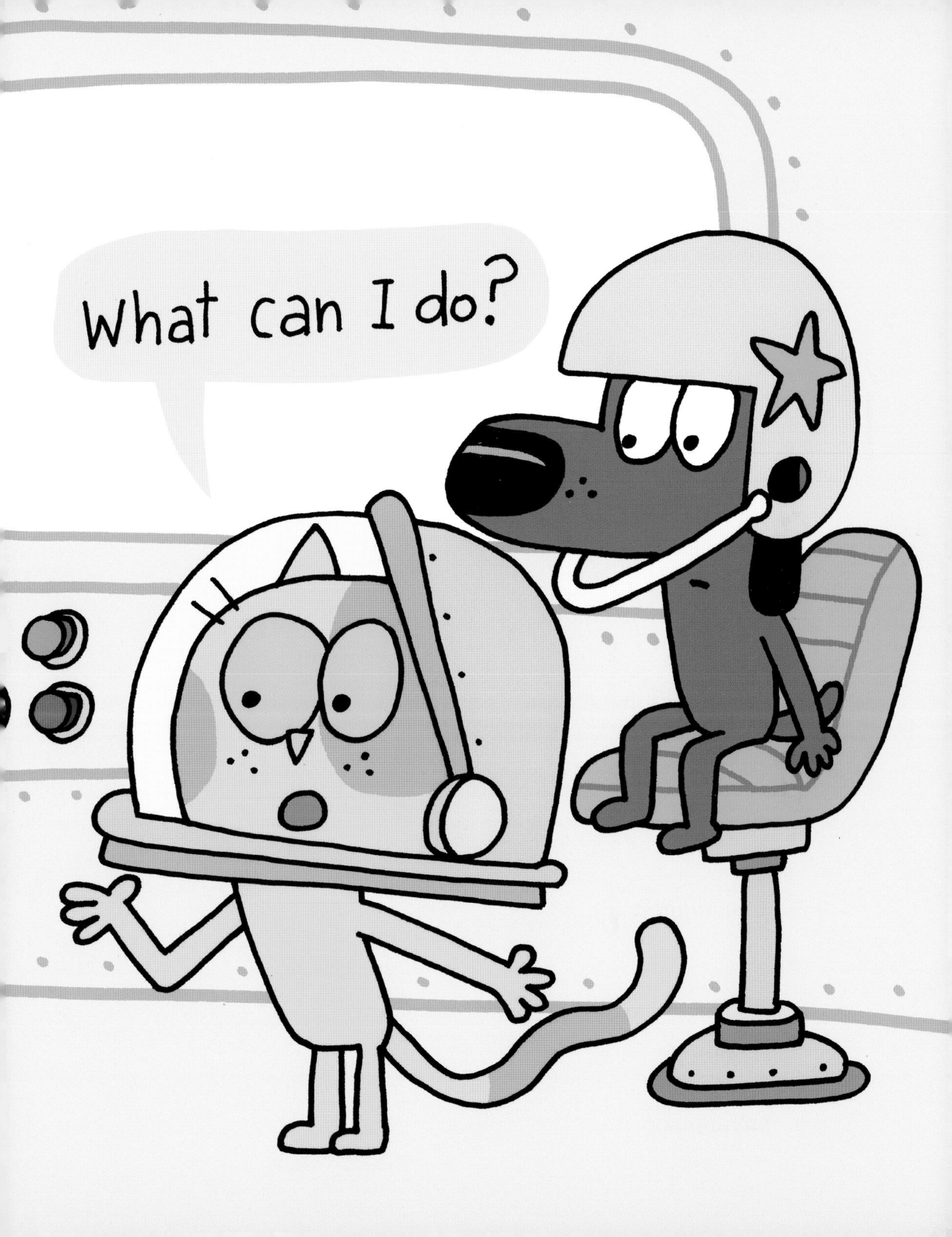
What can I do?

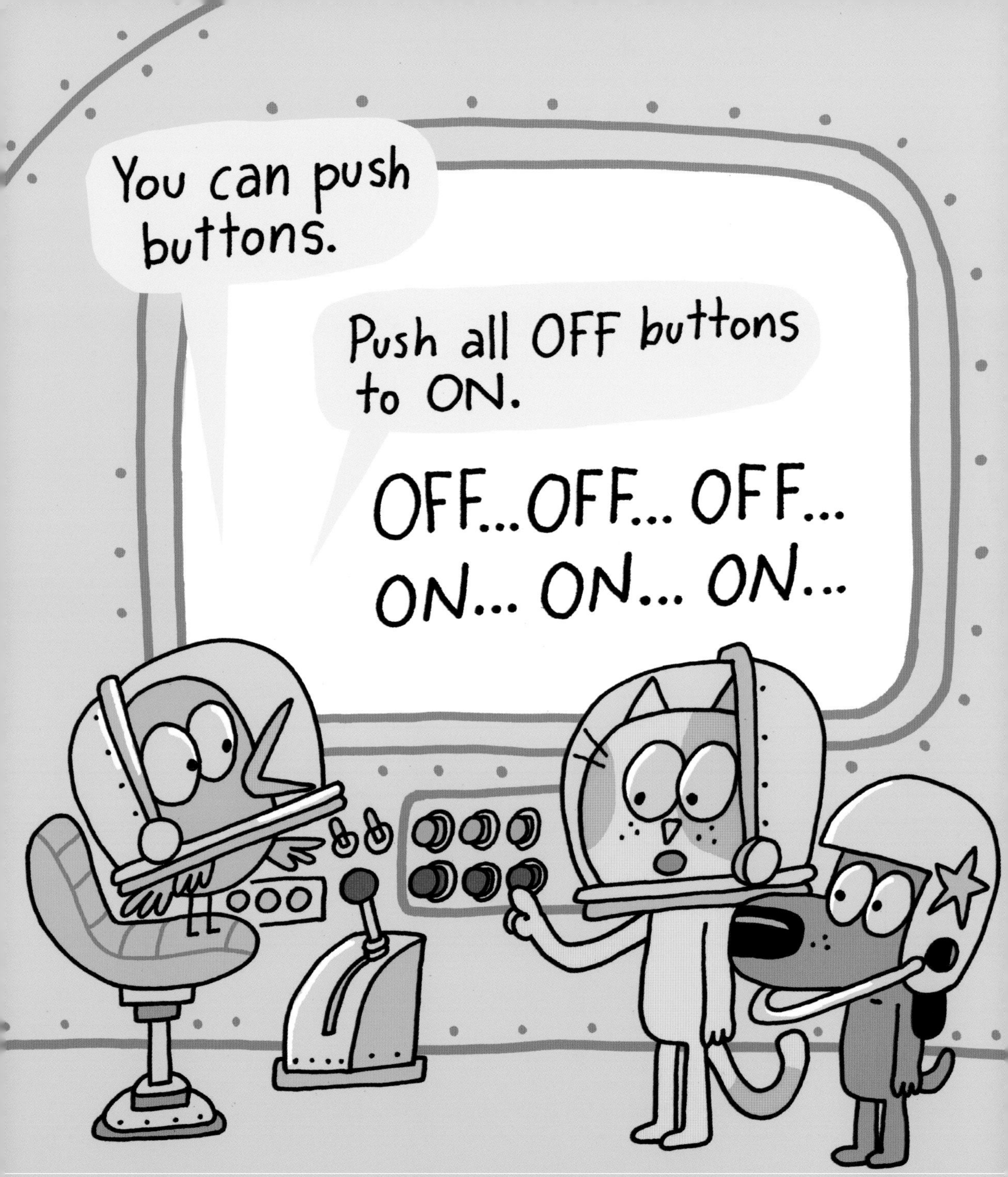
You can push buttons.
Push all OFF buttons to ON.
OFF...OFF... OFF...
ON... ON... ON...

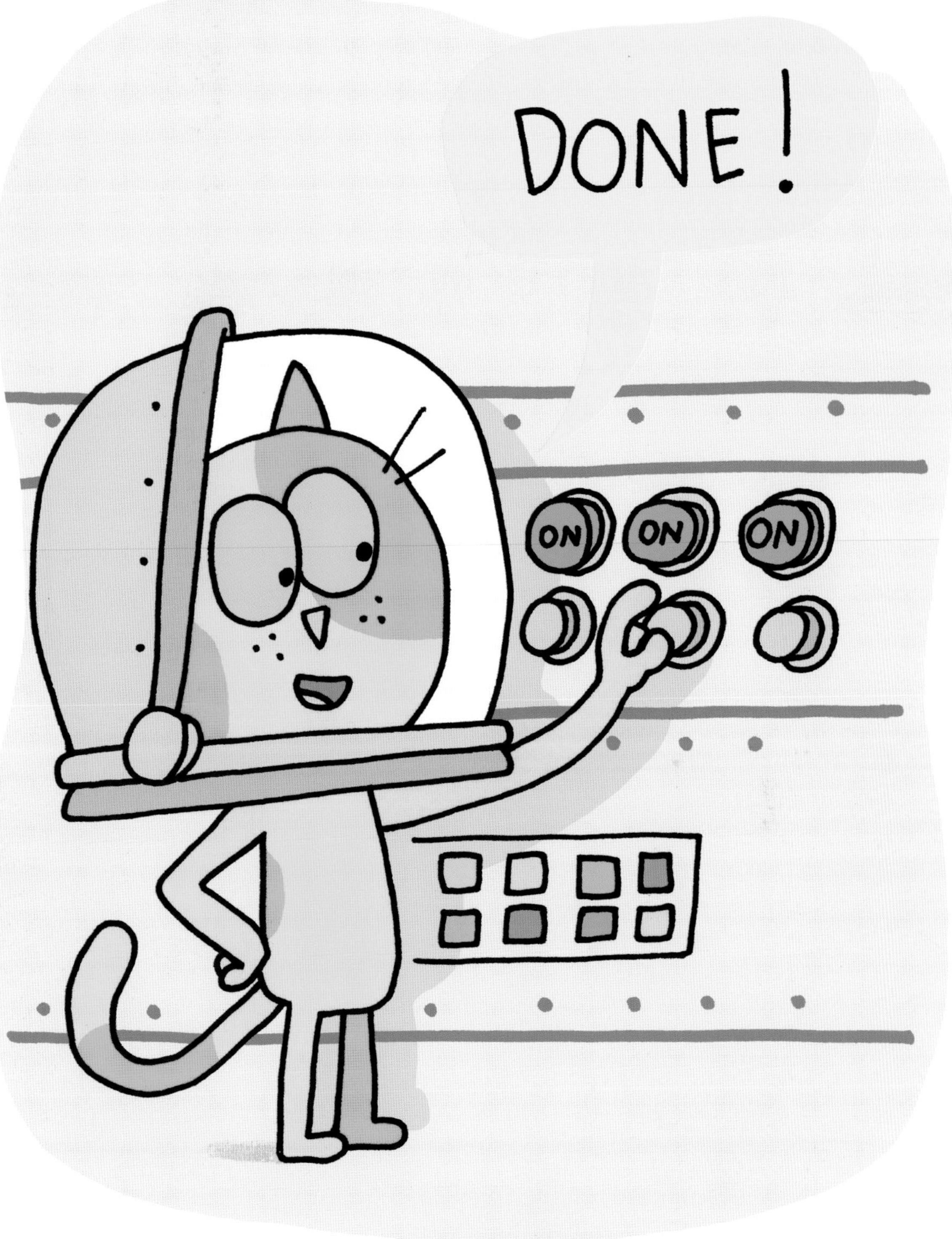
DONE!
ON
ON
ON

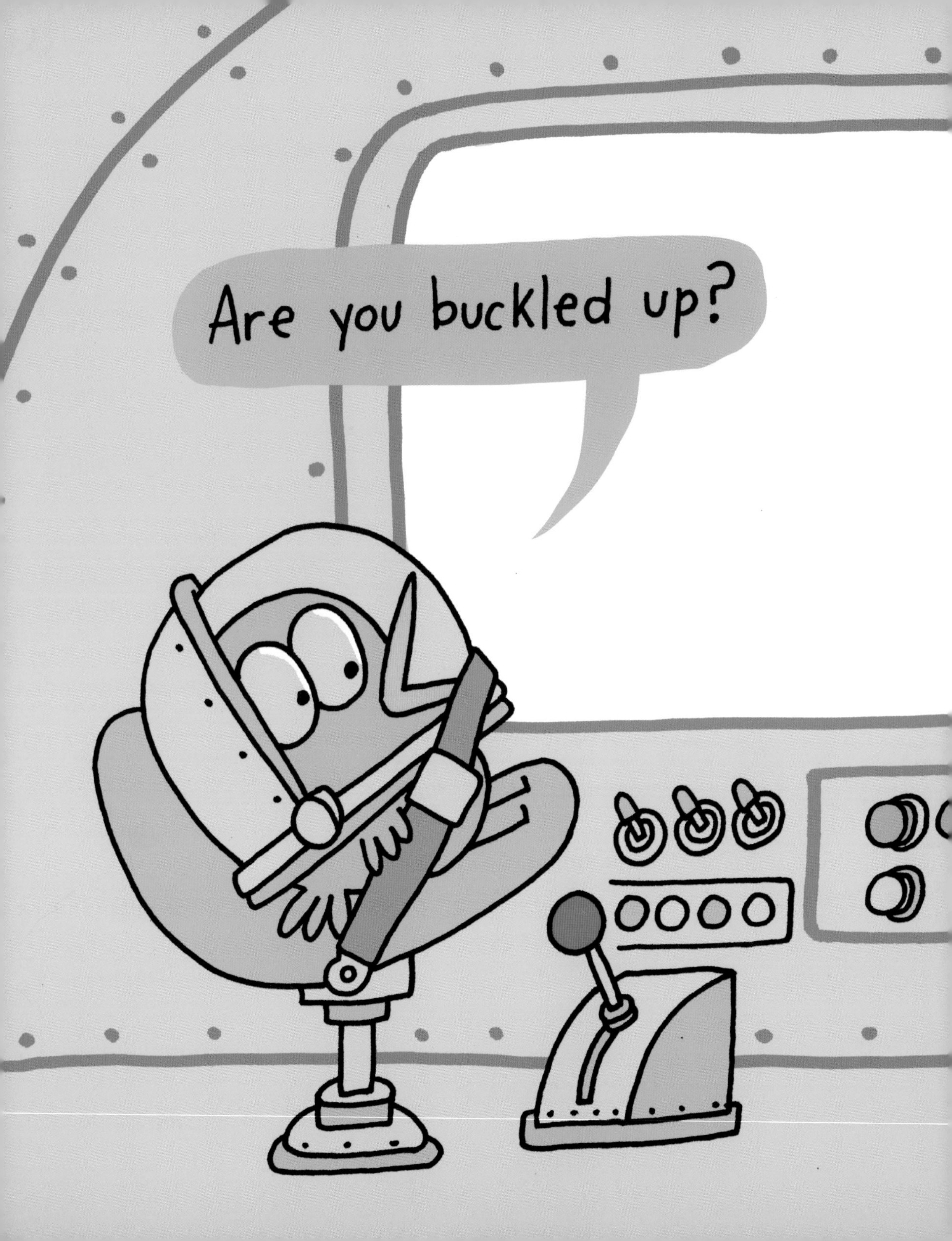
Are you buckled up?

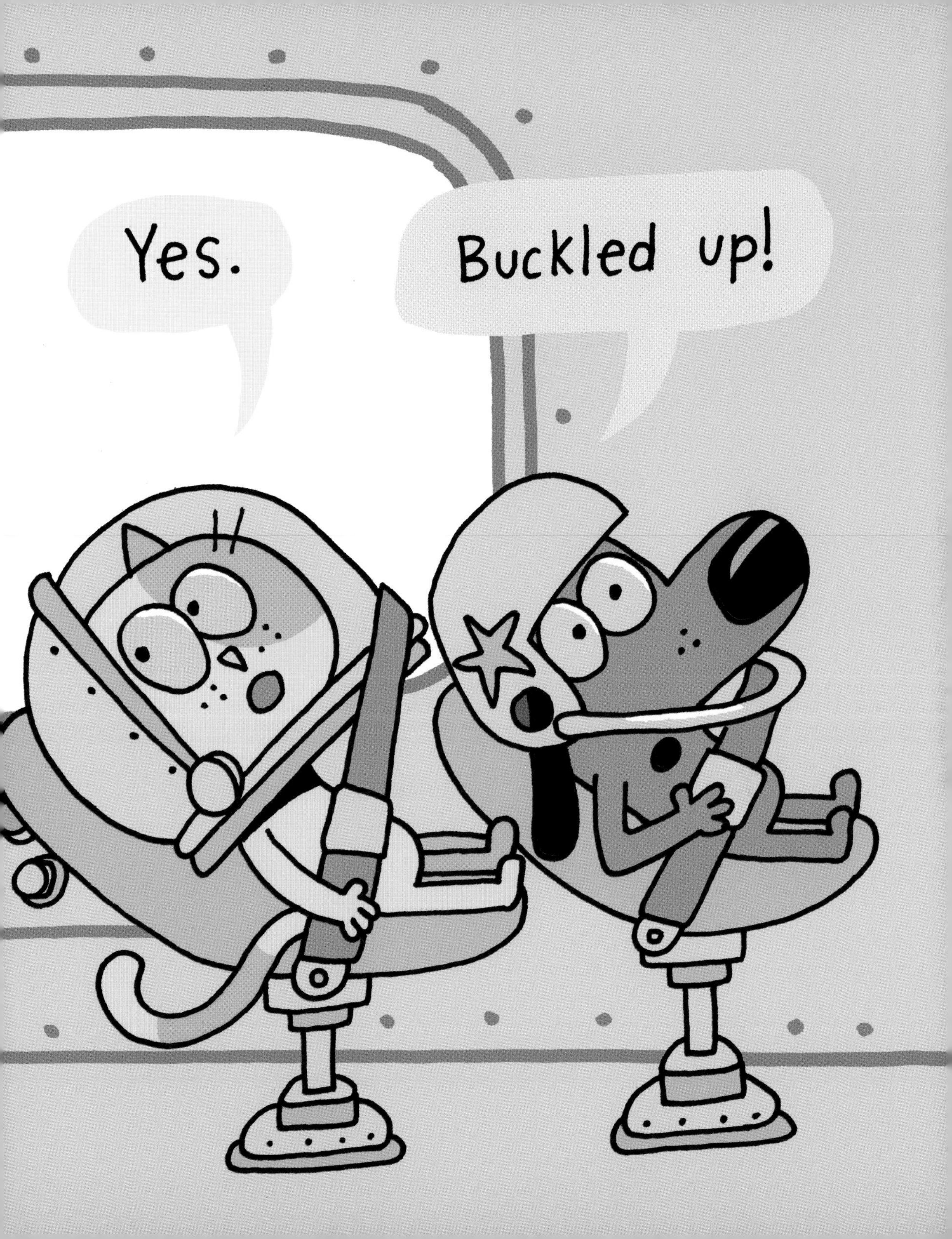
Yes.
Buckled up!

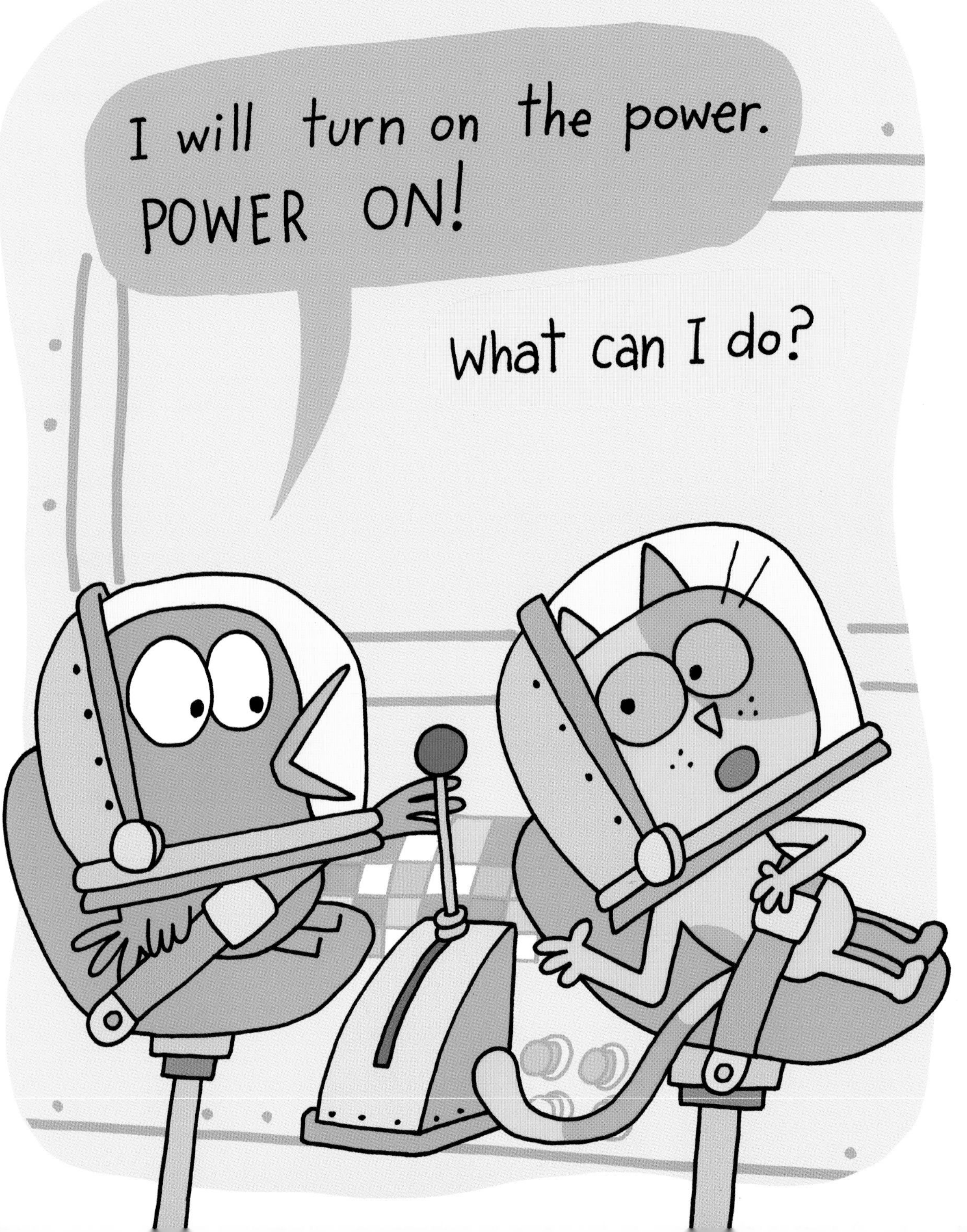
I will turn on the power.
POWER ON!
What can I do?

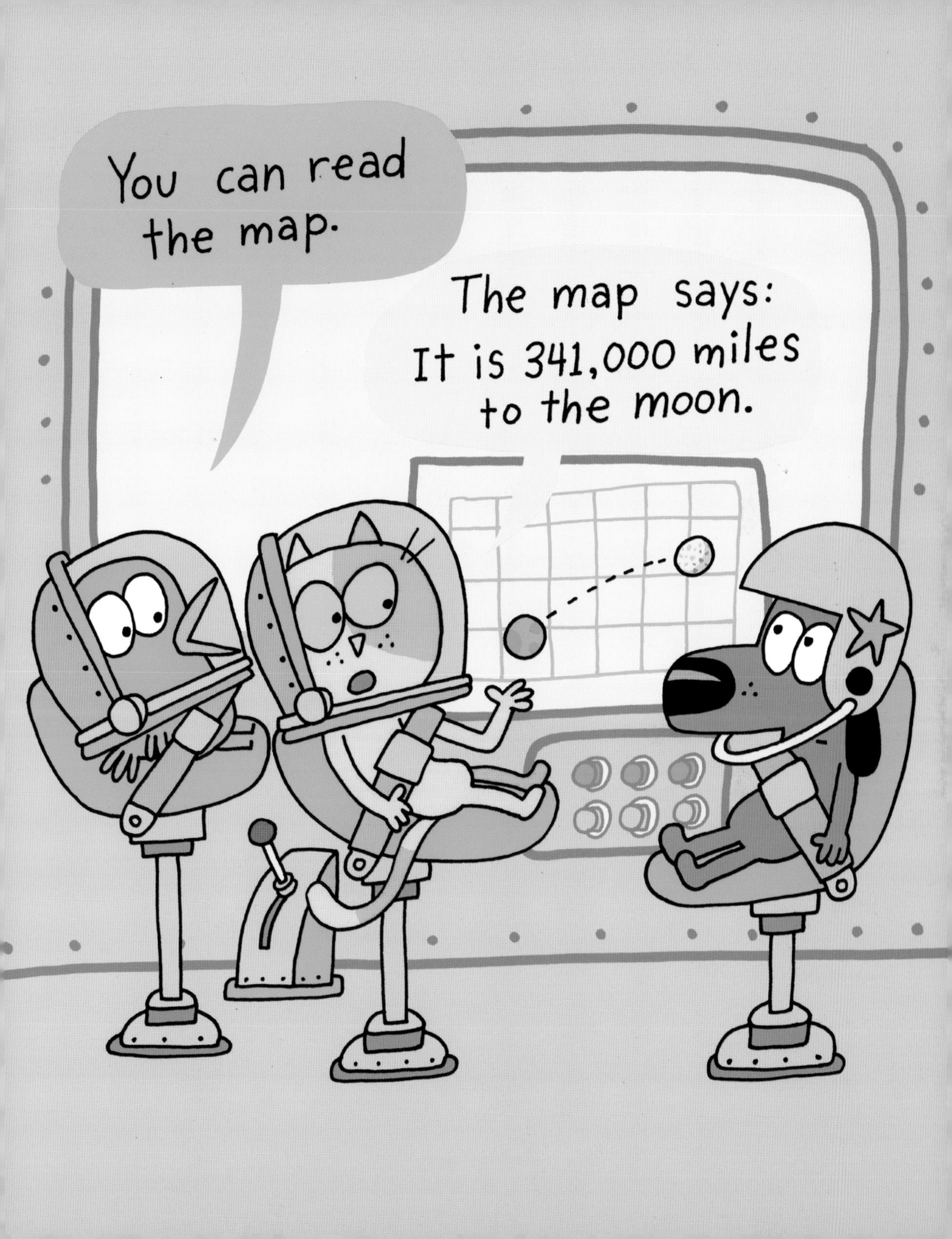
You can read the map.
The map says: It is 341,000 miles to the moon.

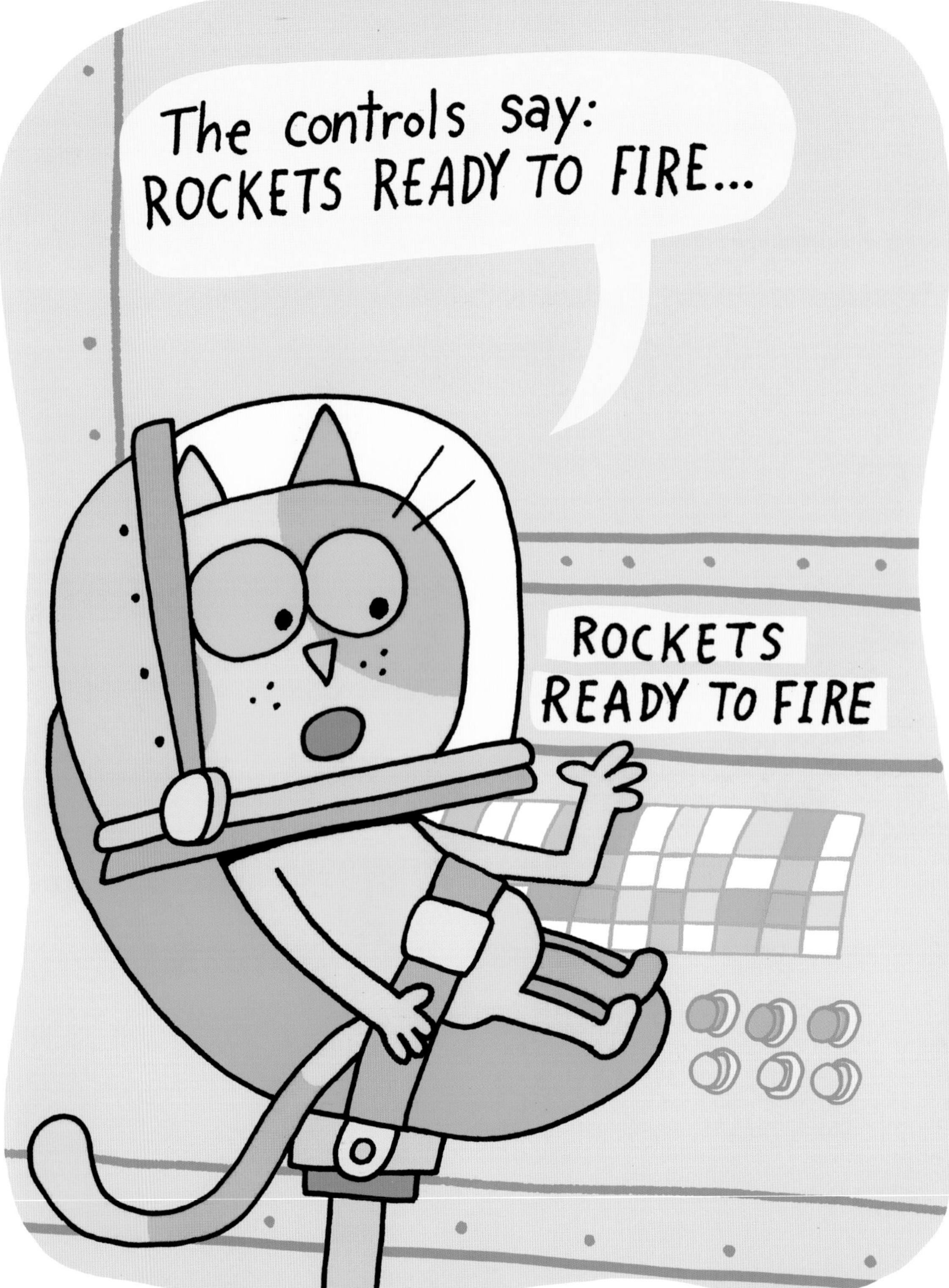
The controls say:
ROCKETS READY TO FIRE...
ROCKETS
READY TO FIRE

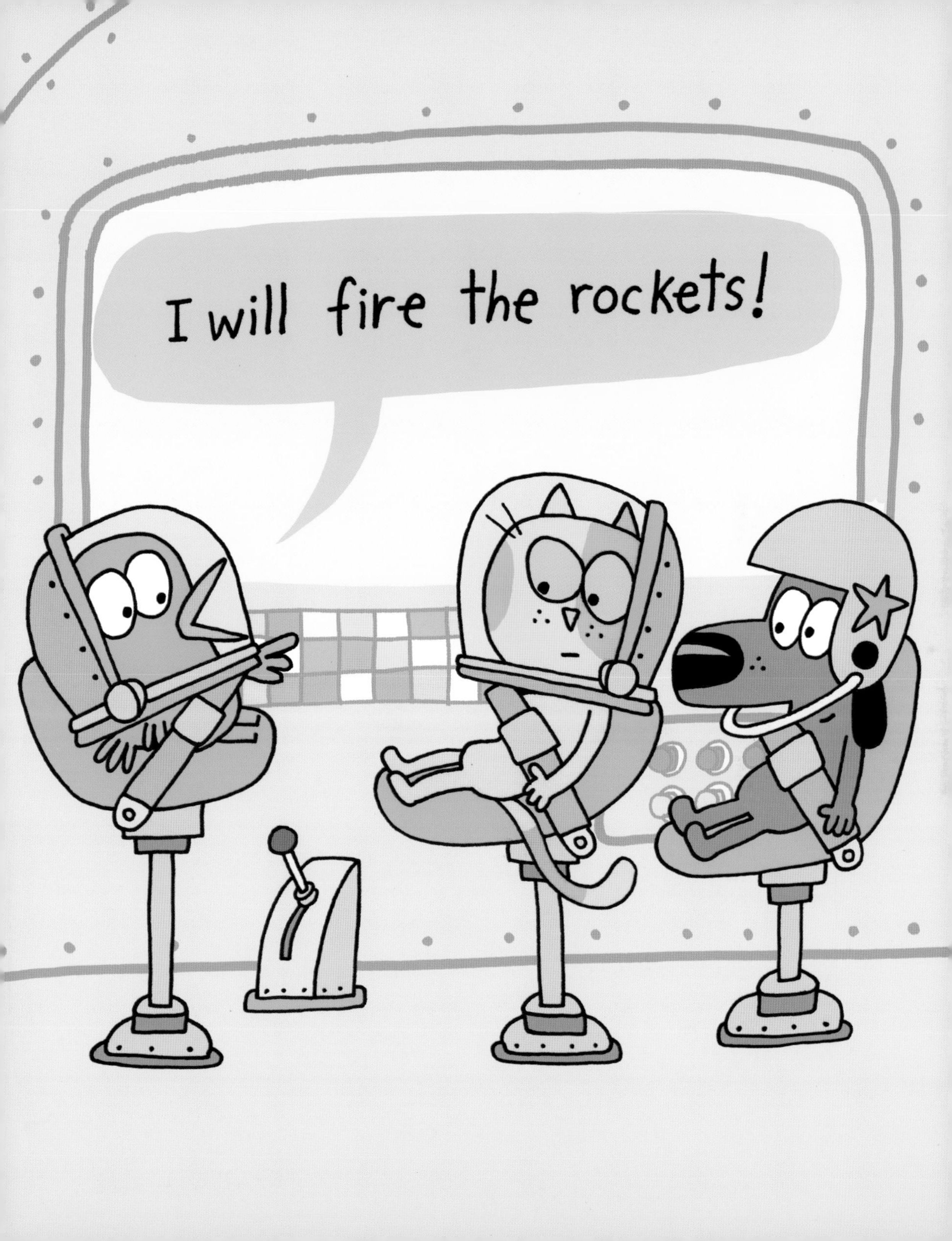
I will fire the rockets!

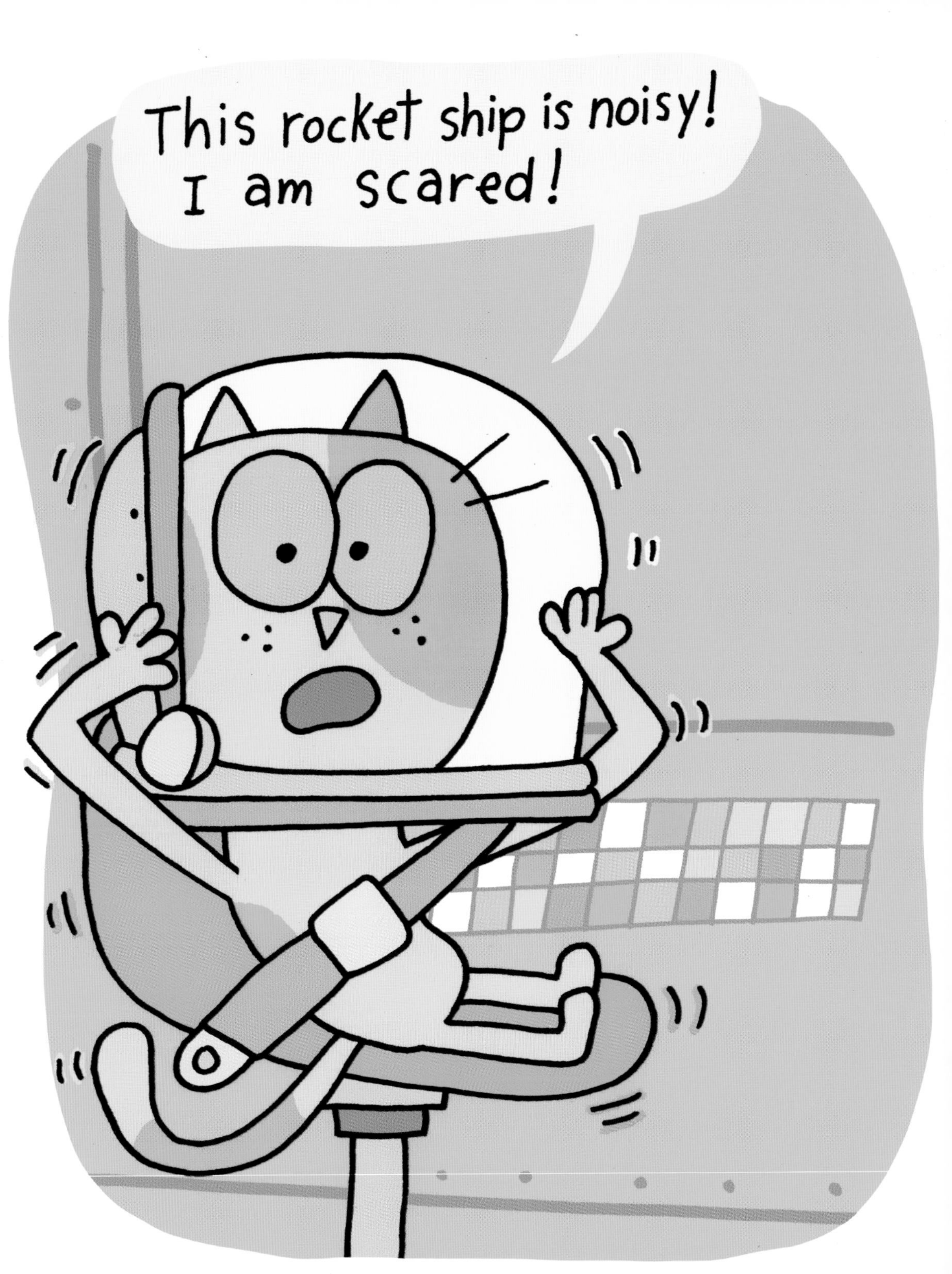
This rocket ship is noisy! I am scared!

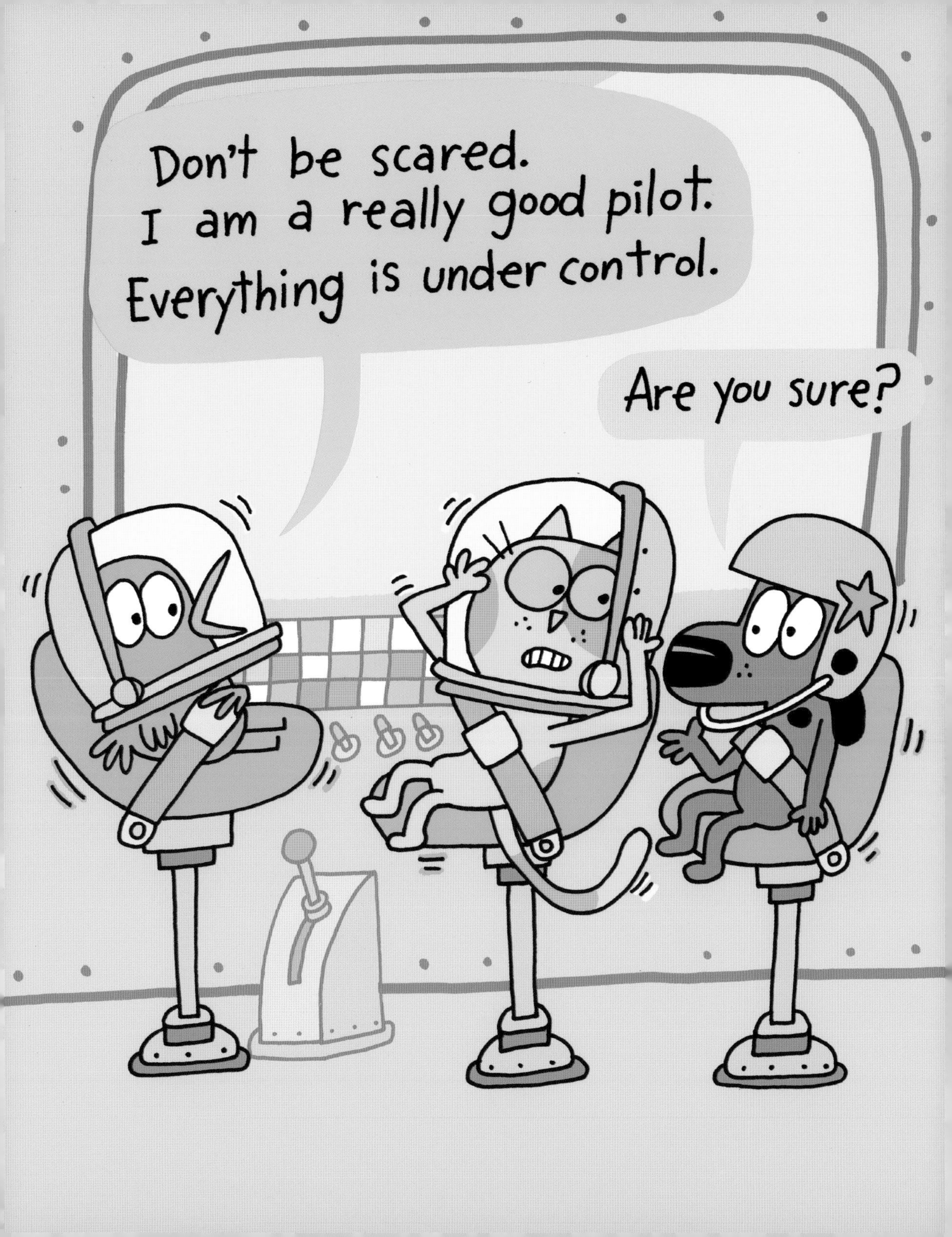
Don't be scared. I am a really good pilot. Everything is under control.
Are you sure?

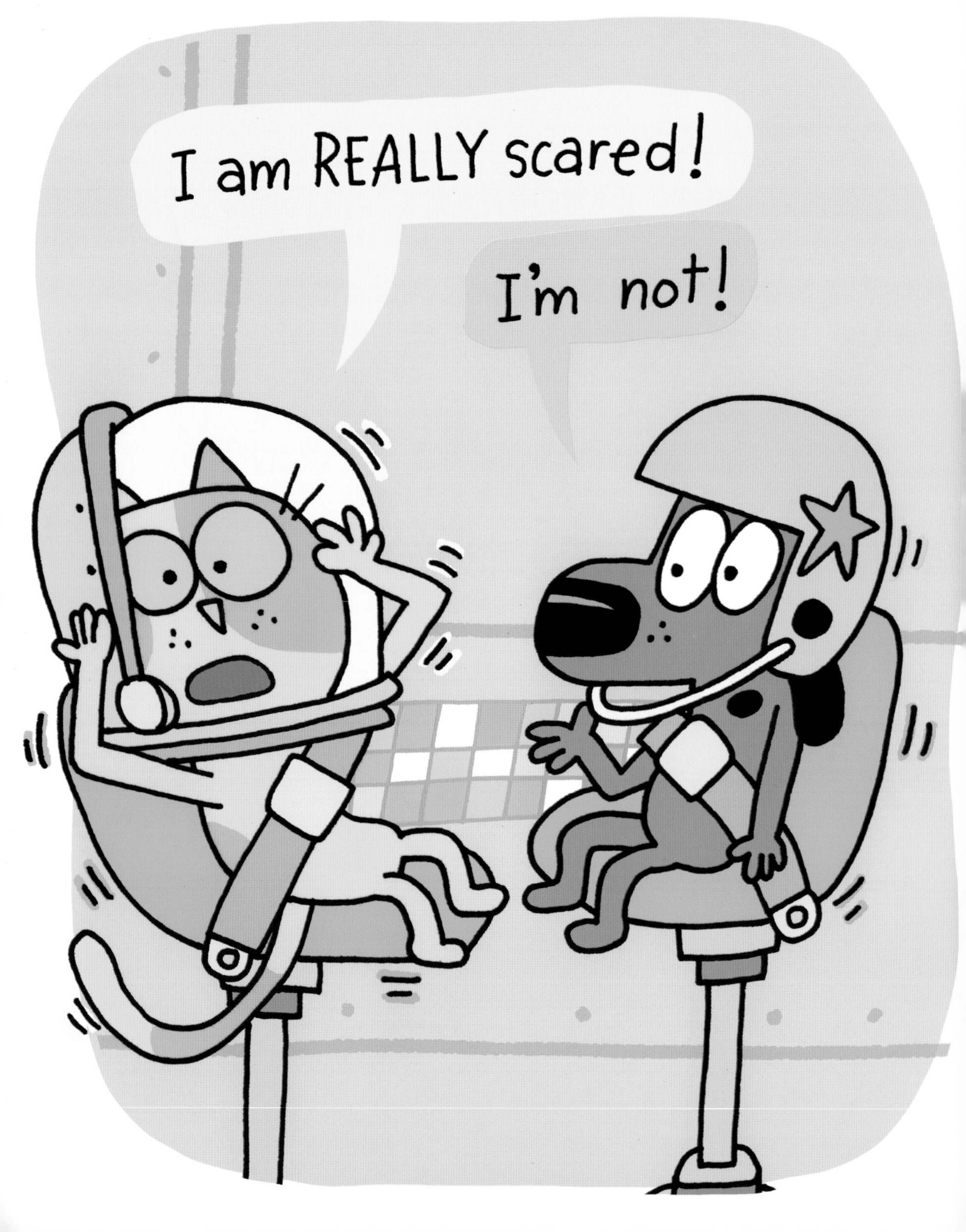
I am REALLY scared!
I'm not!

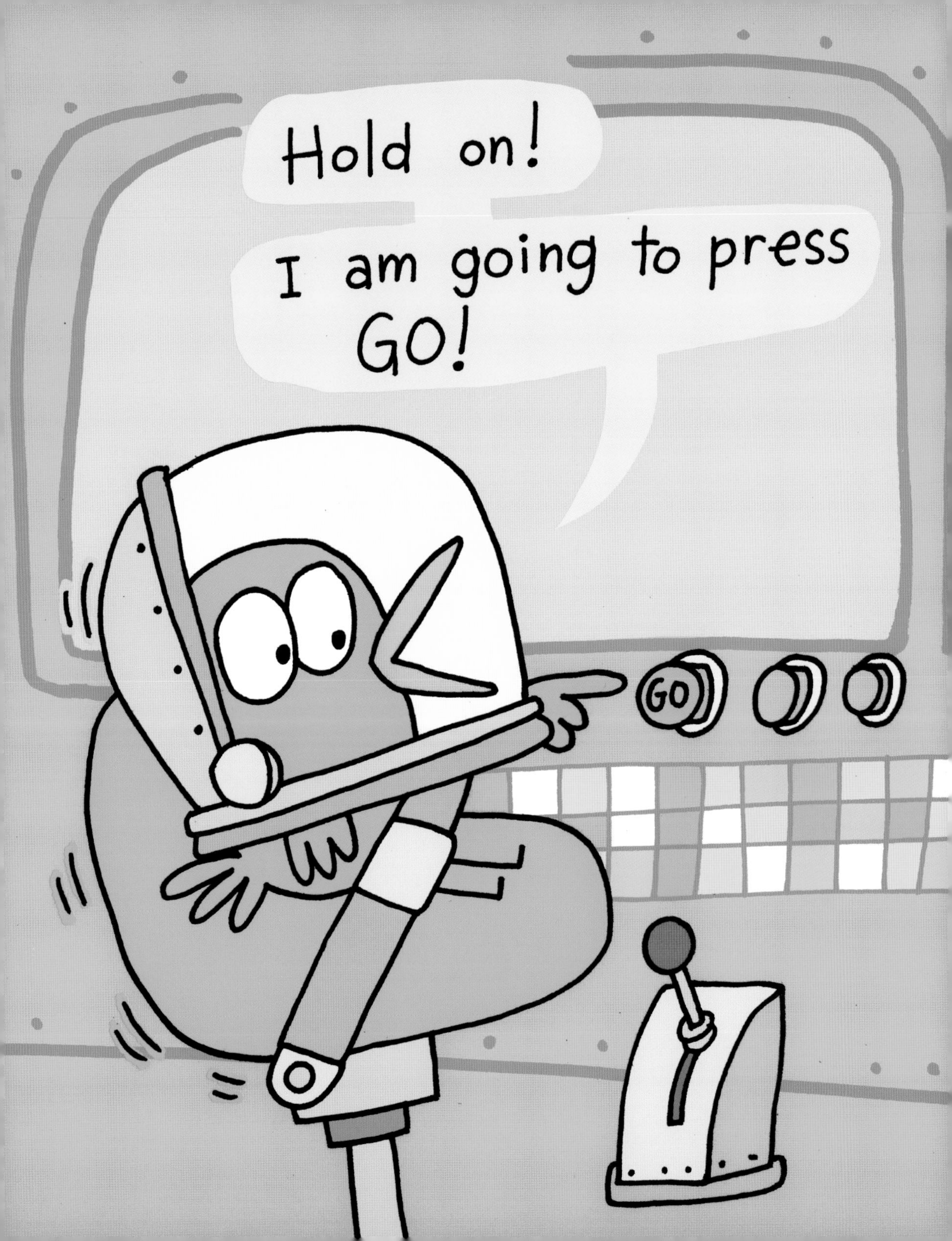
Hold on!
I am going to press GO!
GO

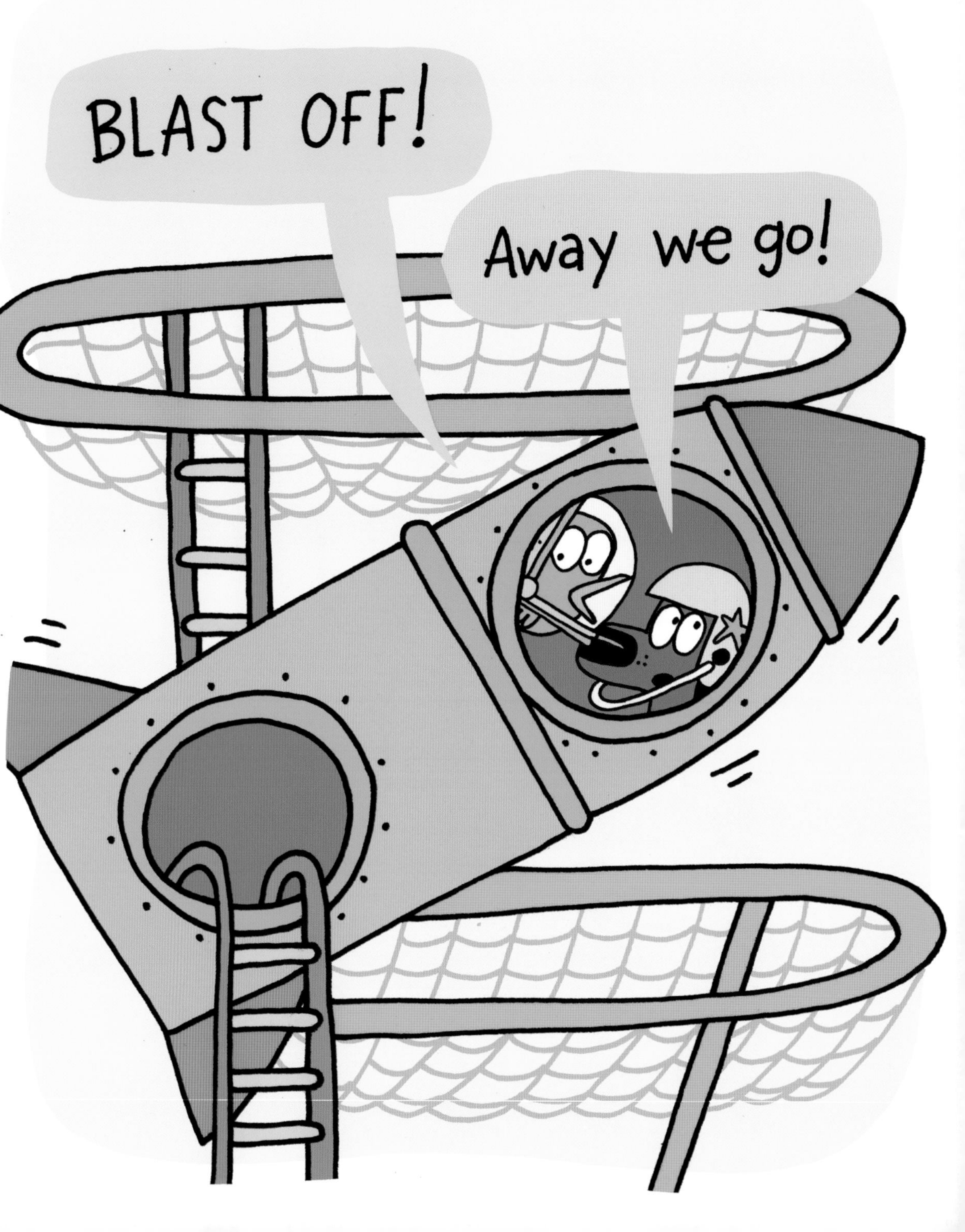
BLAST OFF!
Away we go!

Zoom!
ZOOM AWAY!
ZOOM AWAY... from Earth.

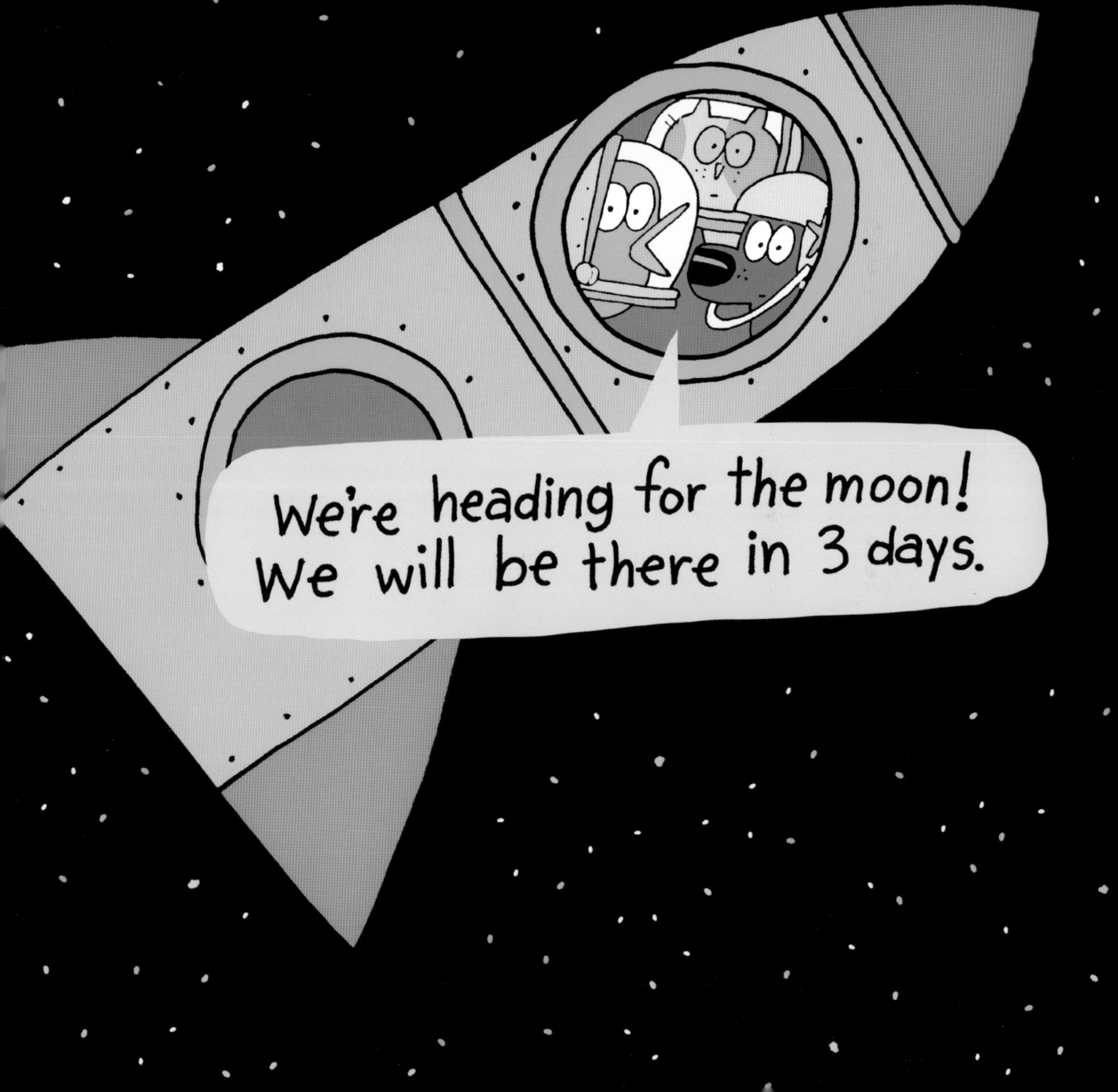

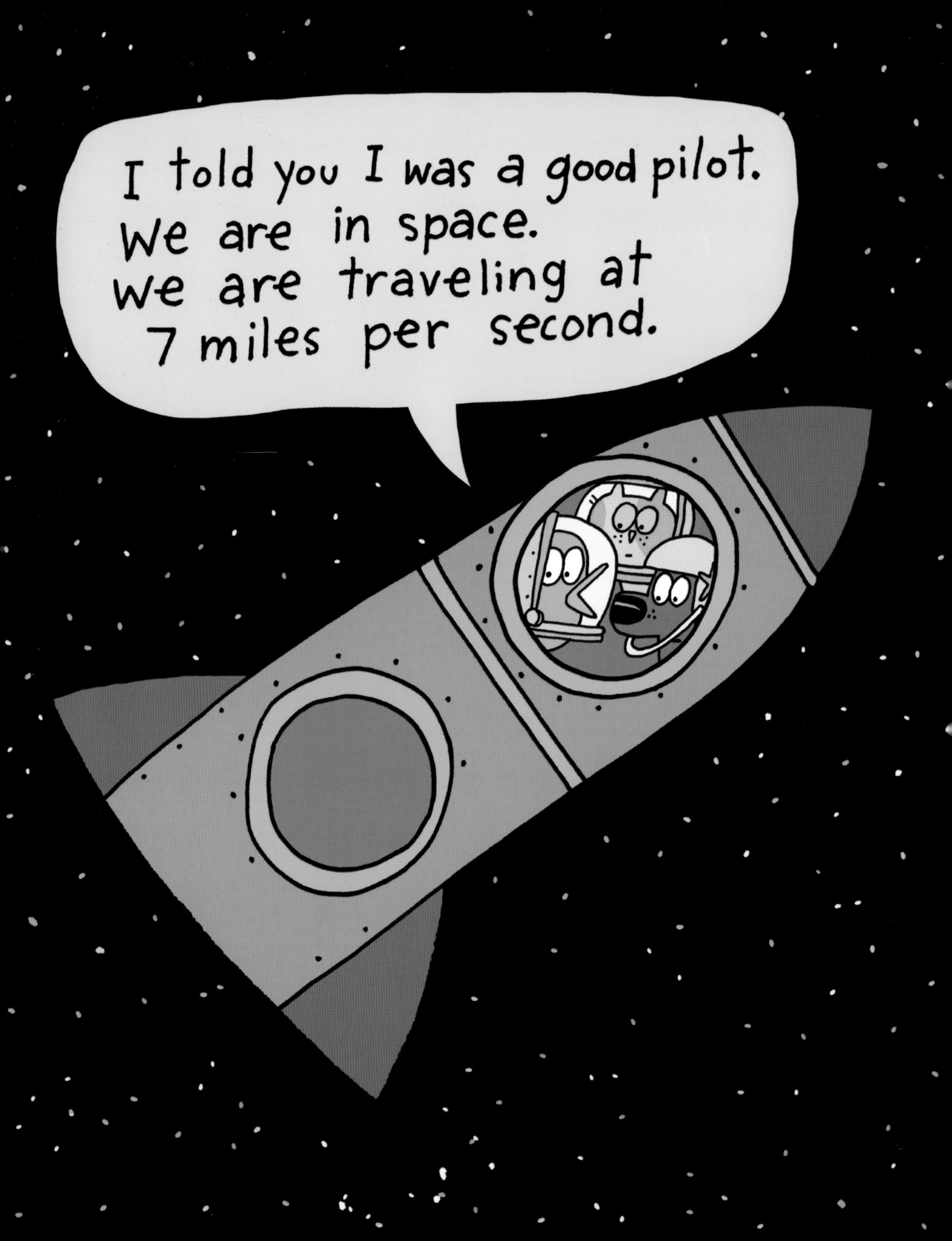
I told you I was a good pilot. We are in space. We are traveling at 7 miles per second.

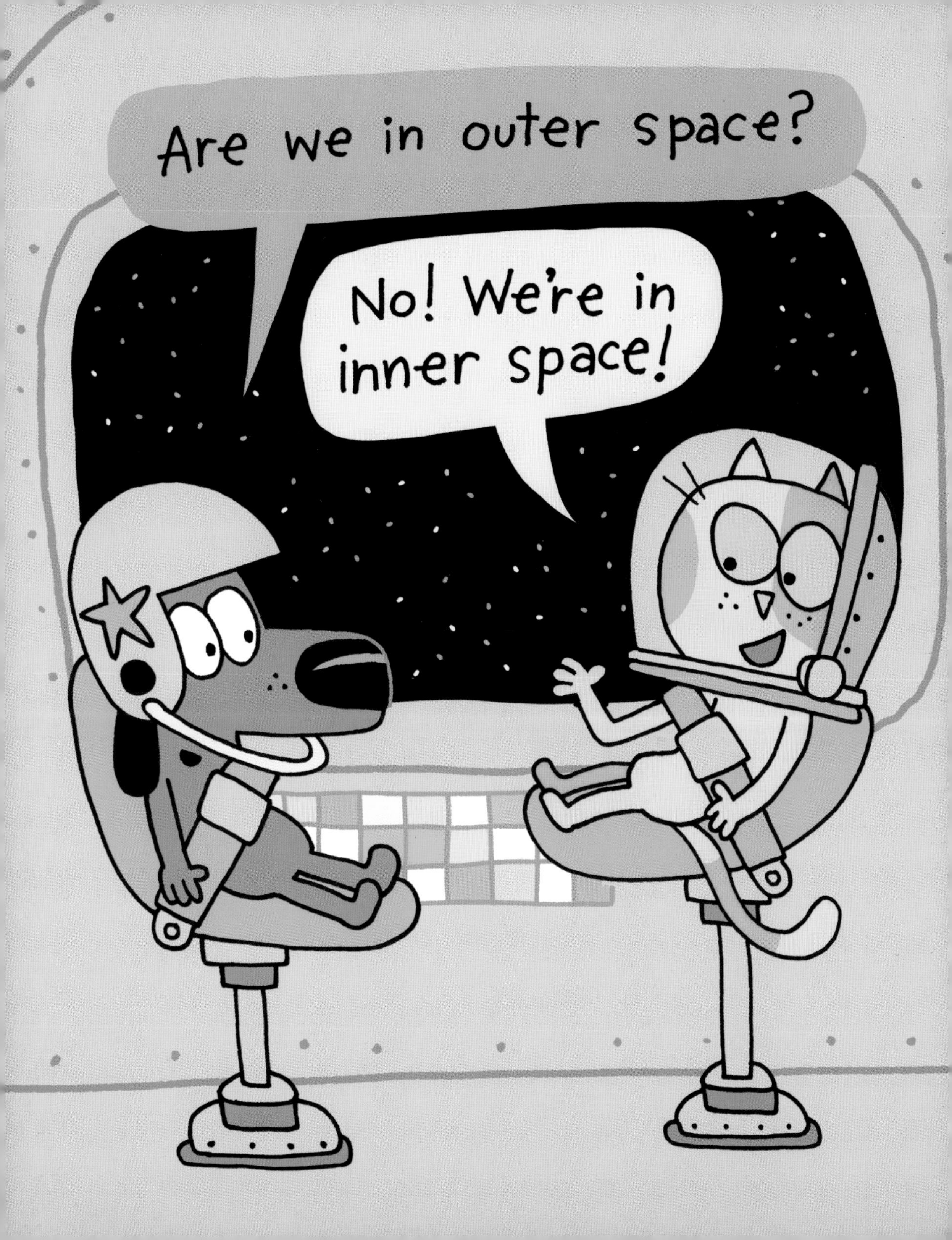
Are we in outer space?
No! We're in inner space!

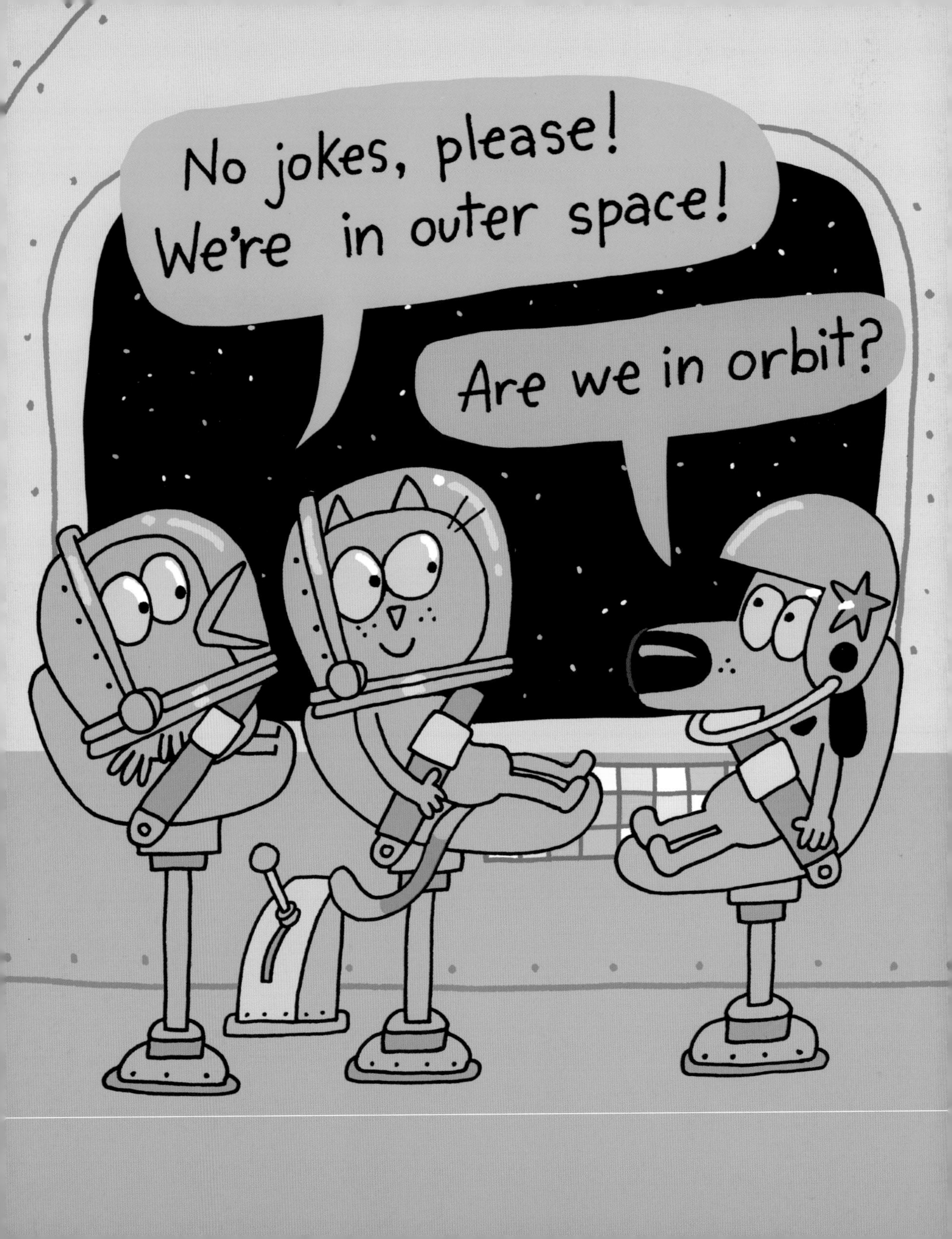
No jokes, please! We're in outer space!
Are we in orbit?

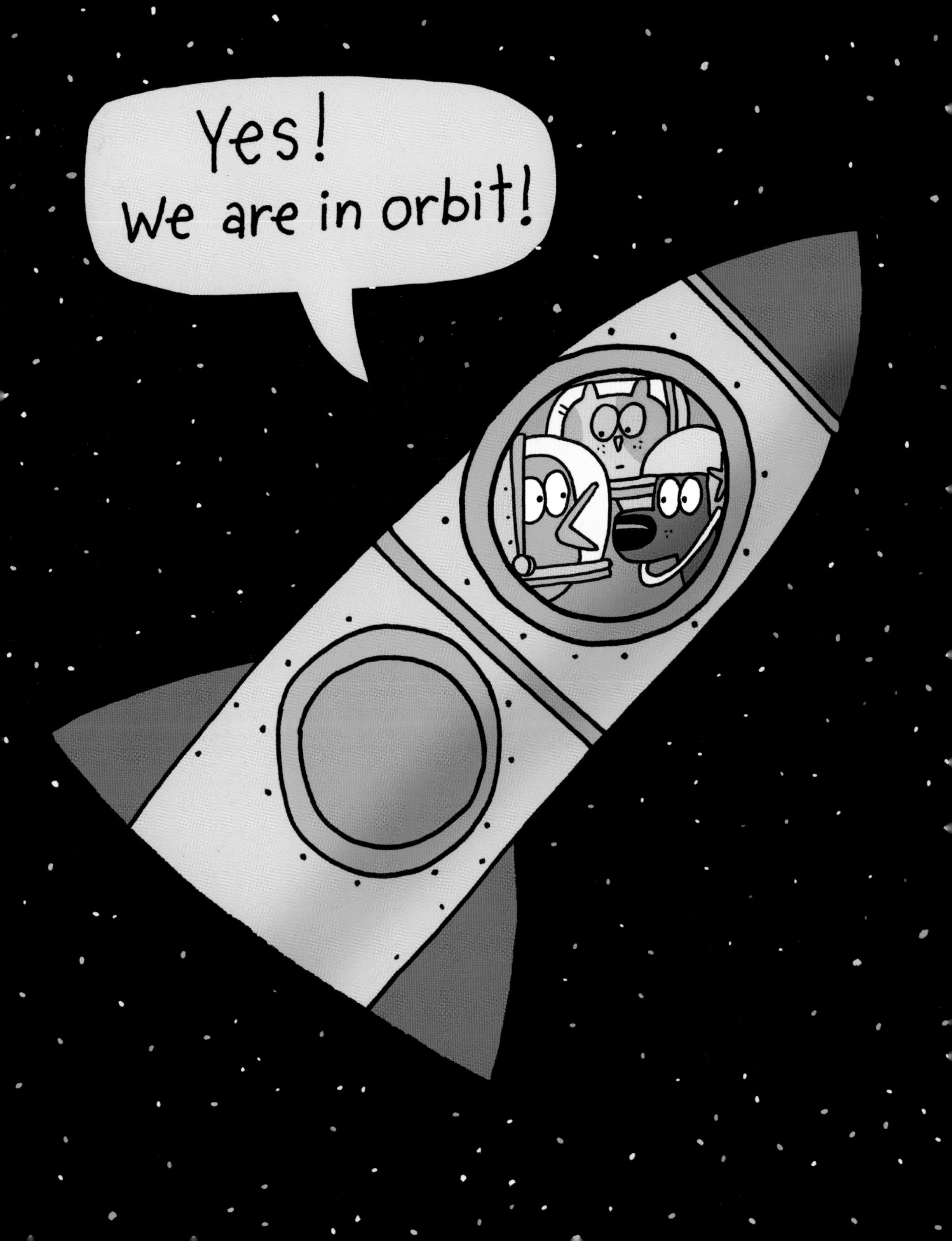
Yes! We are in orbit!

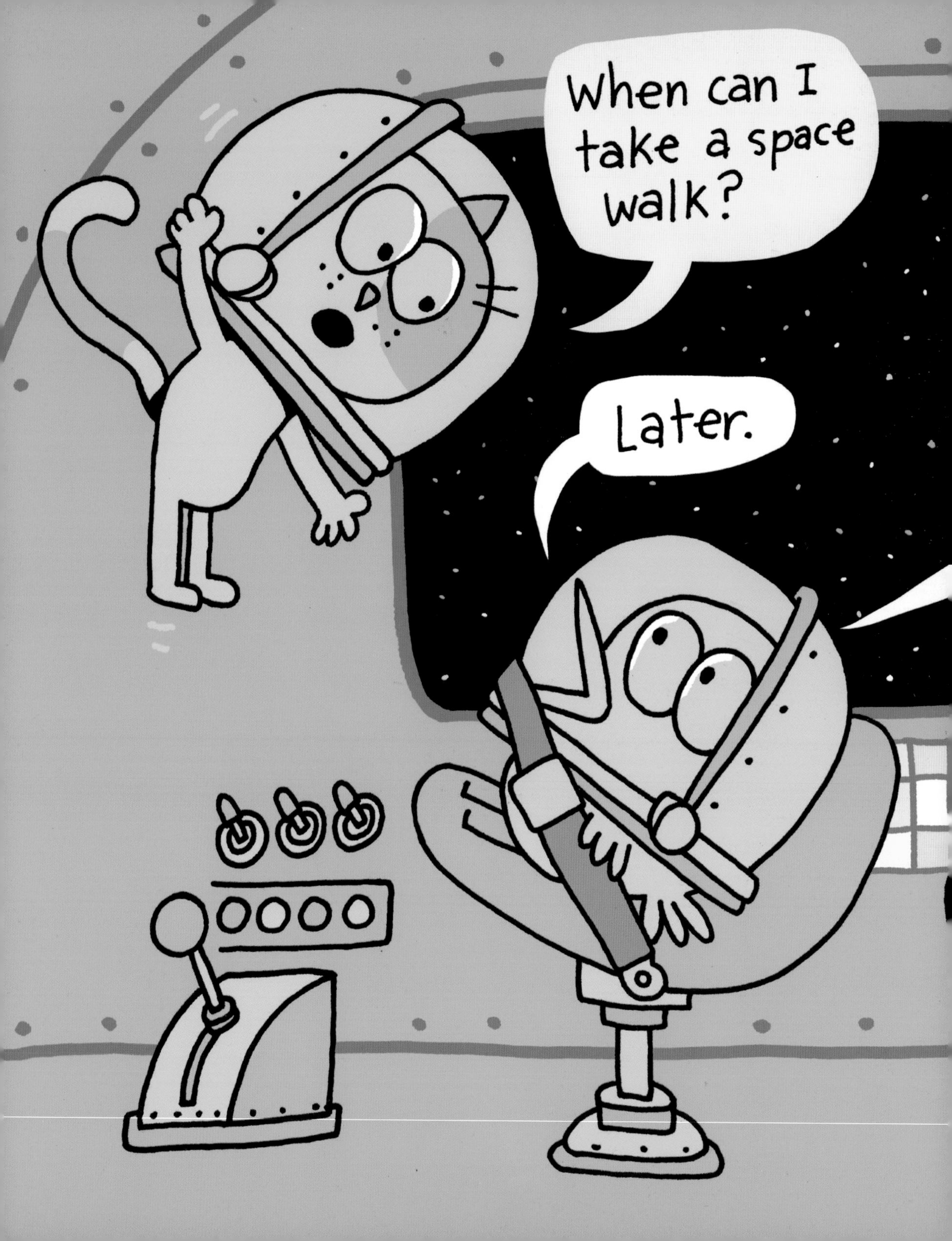
When can I take a space walk?
Later.

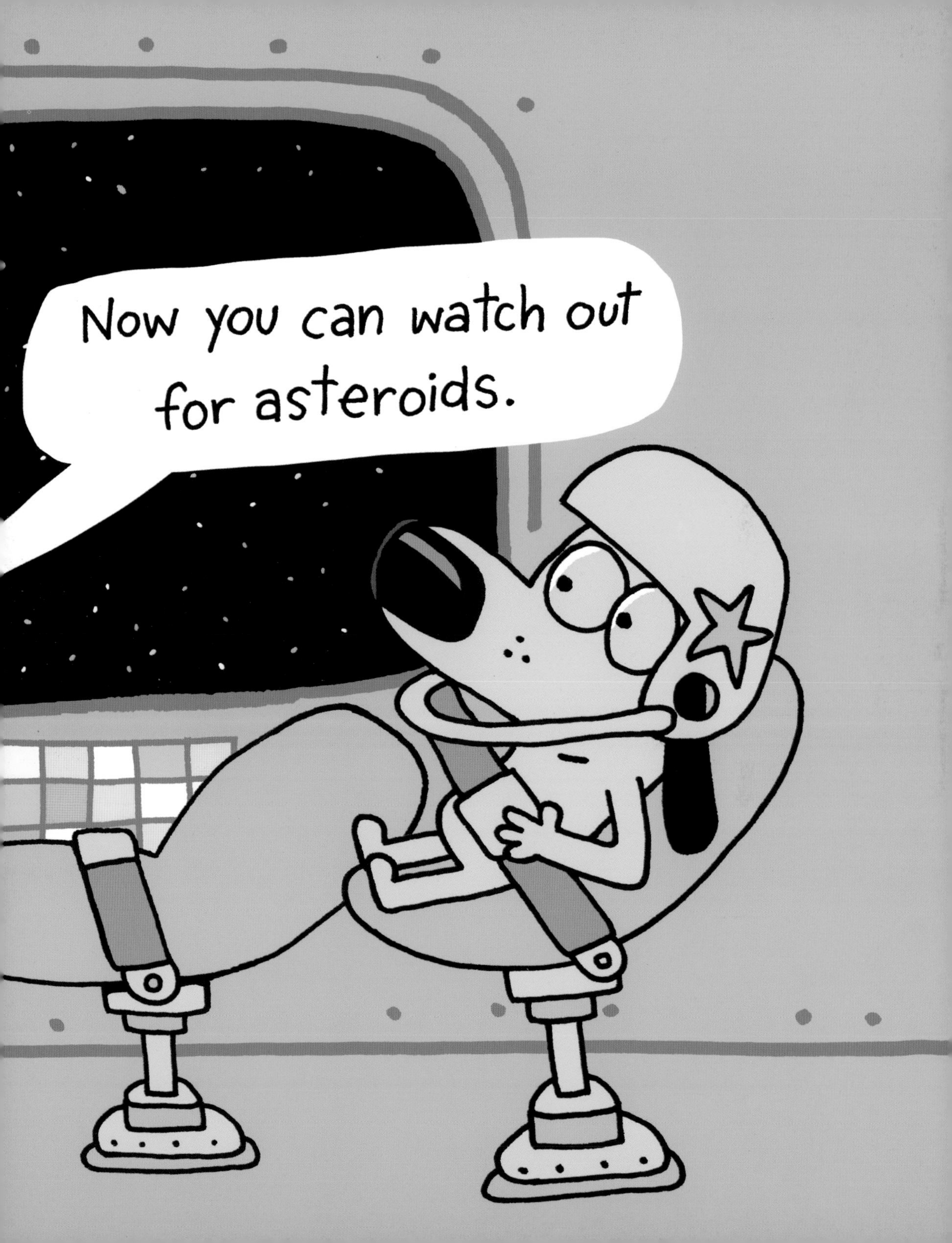
Now you can watch out for asteroids.

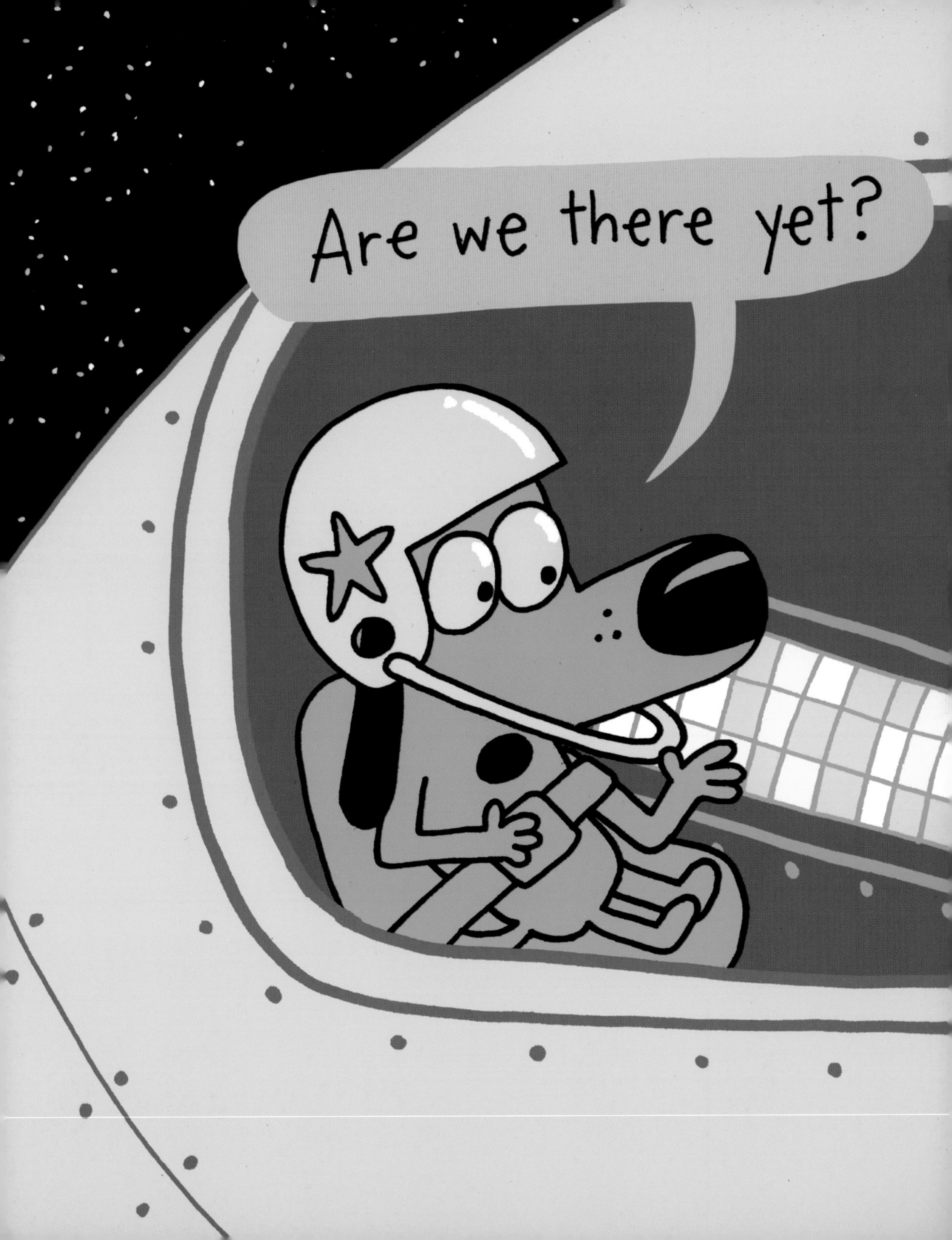
Are we there yet?

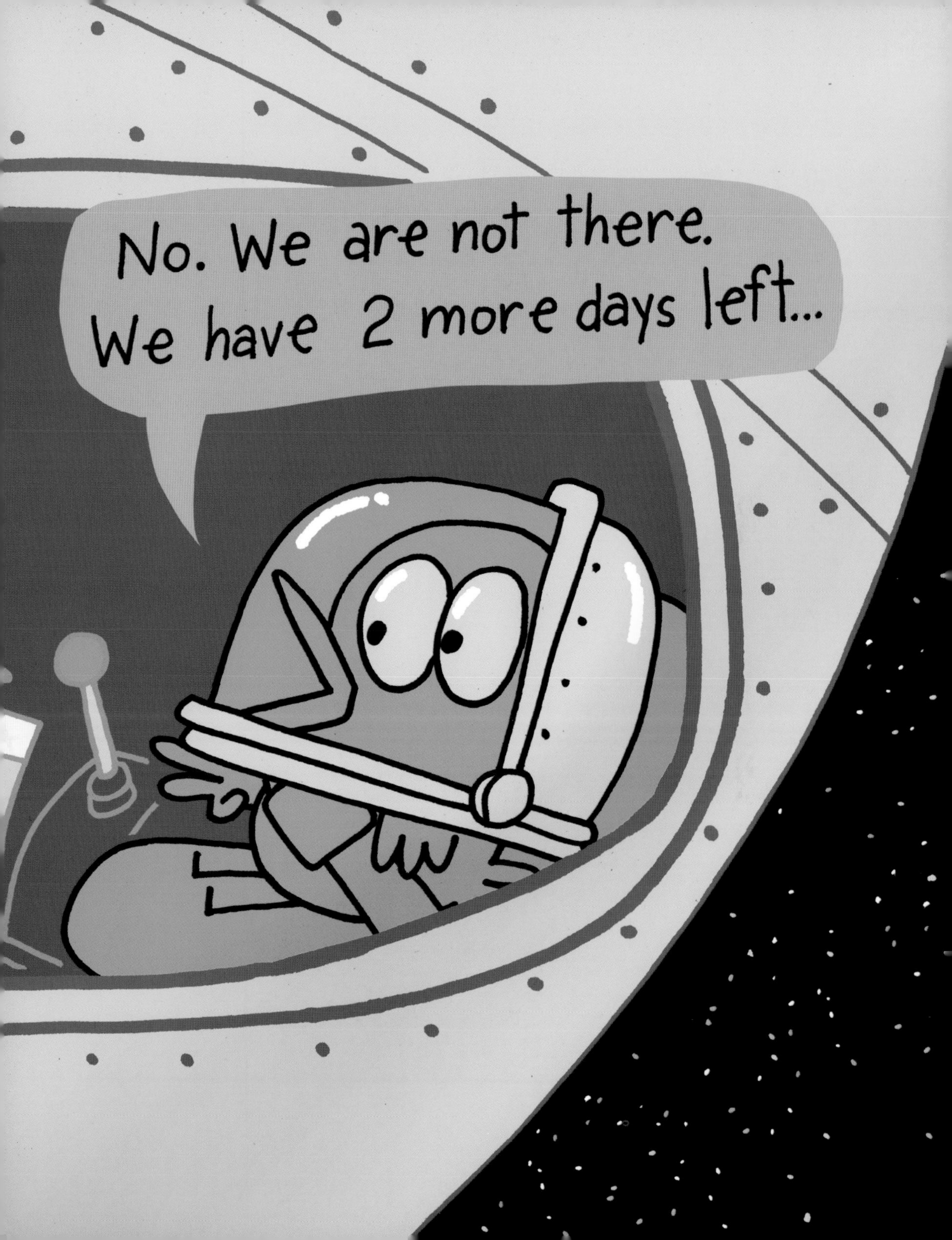
No. We are not there.
We have 2 more days left...

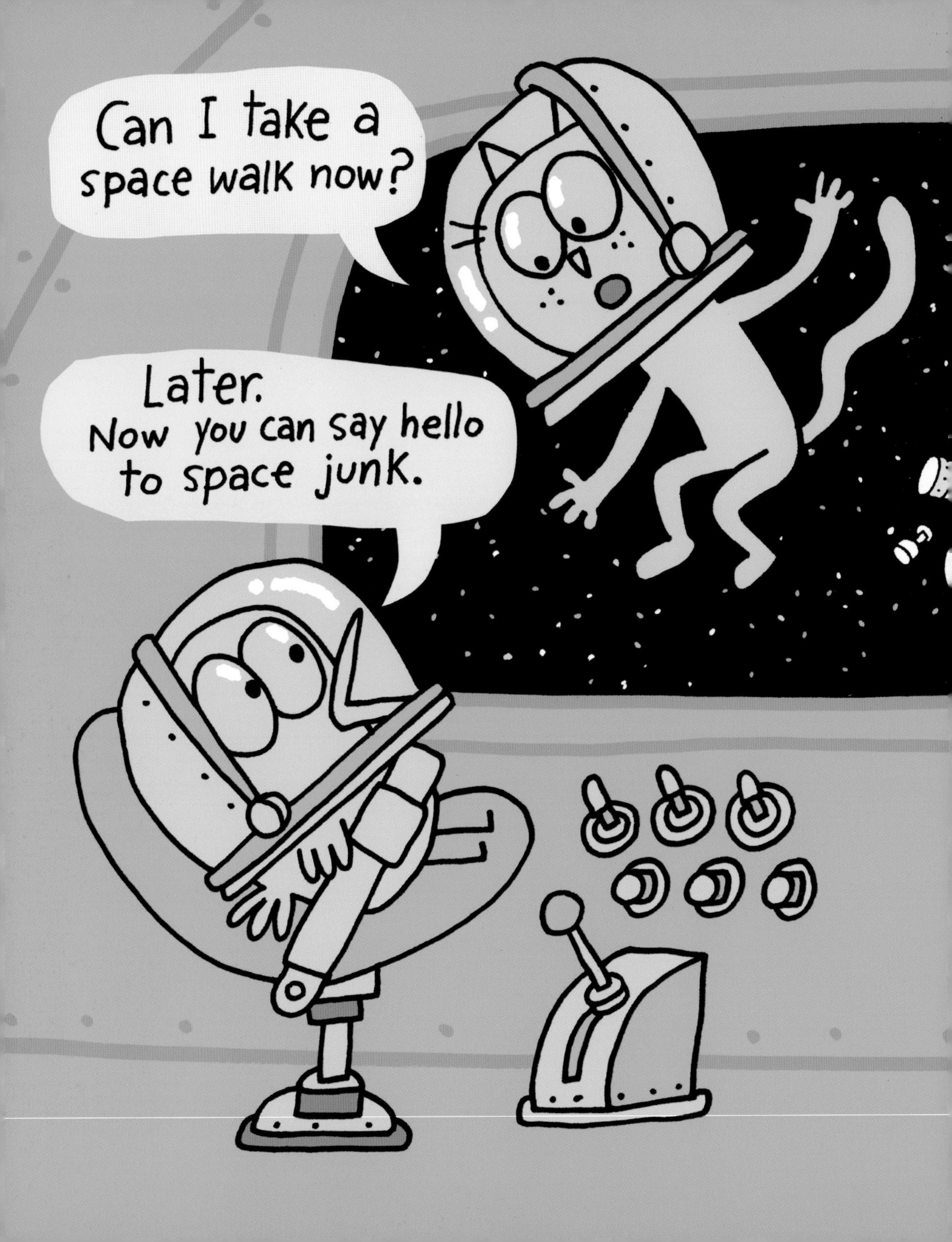
Can I take a space walk now?
Later. Now you can say hello to space junk.

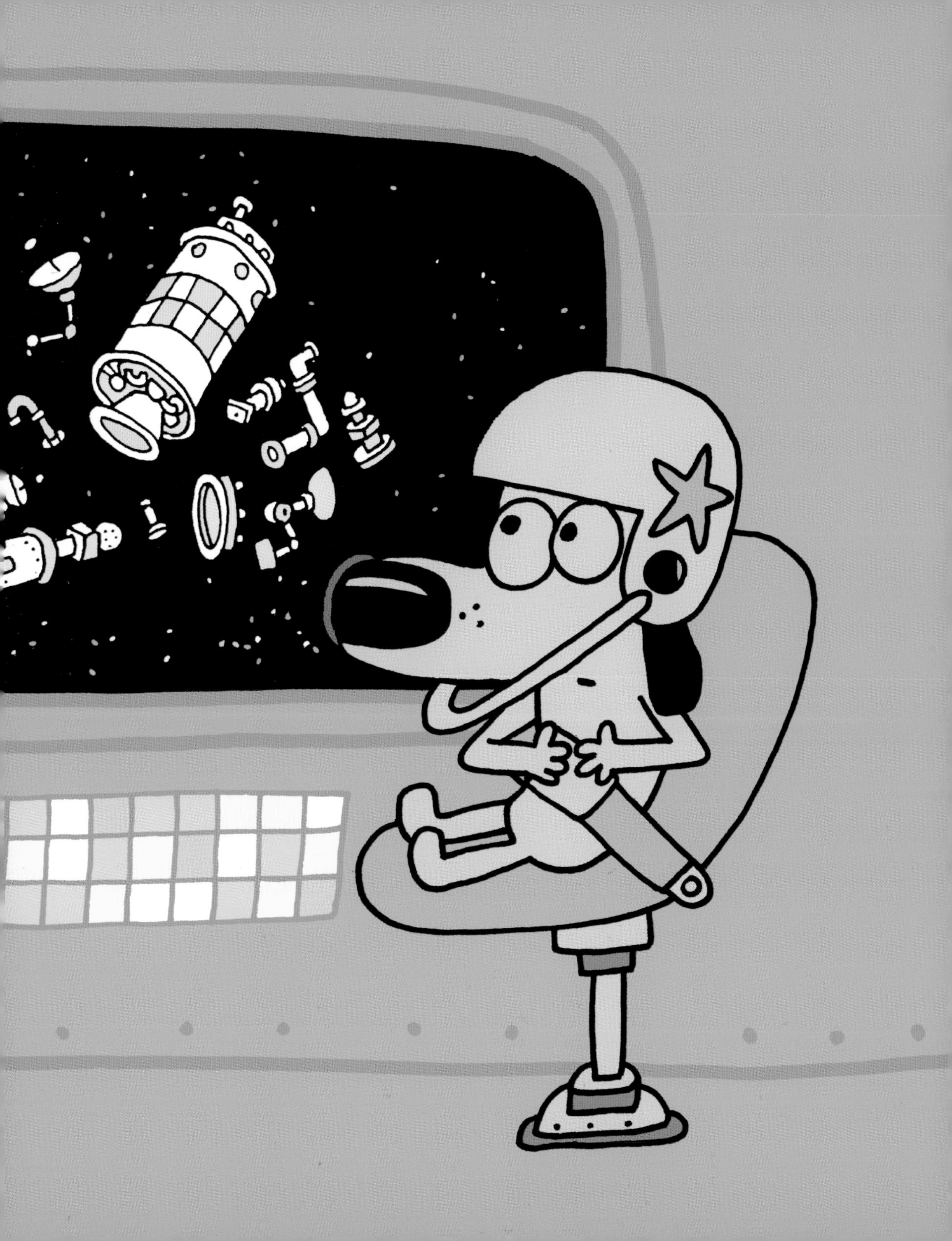

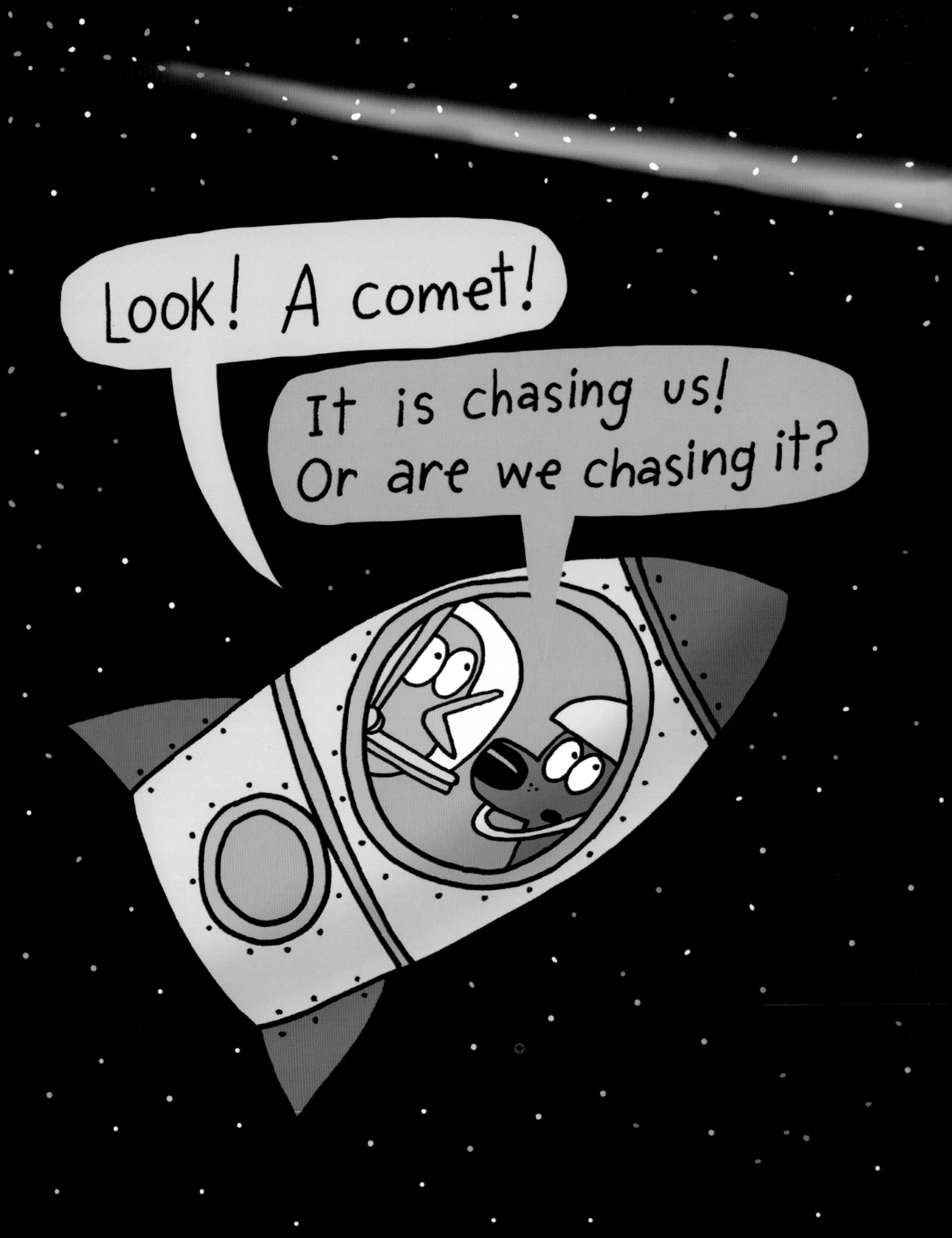
Look! A comet!
It is chasing us! Or are we chasing it?

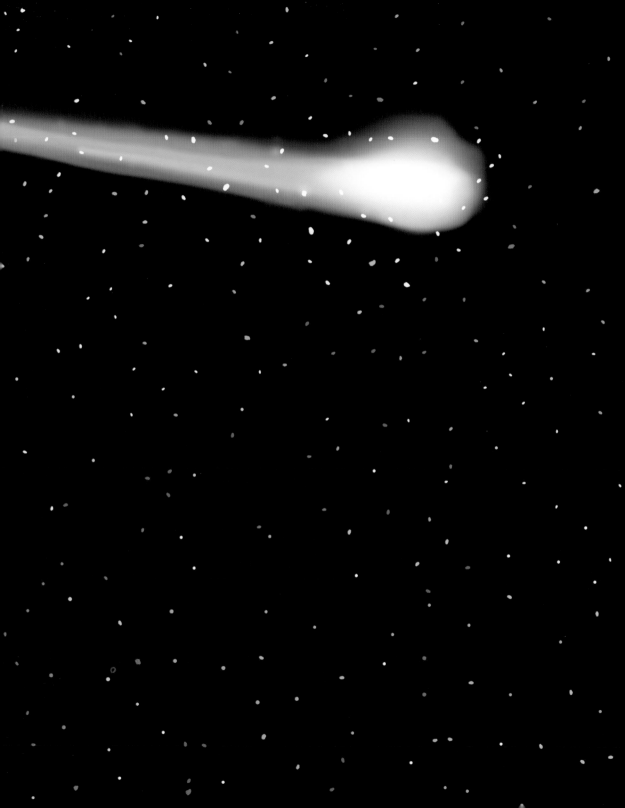

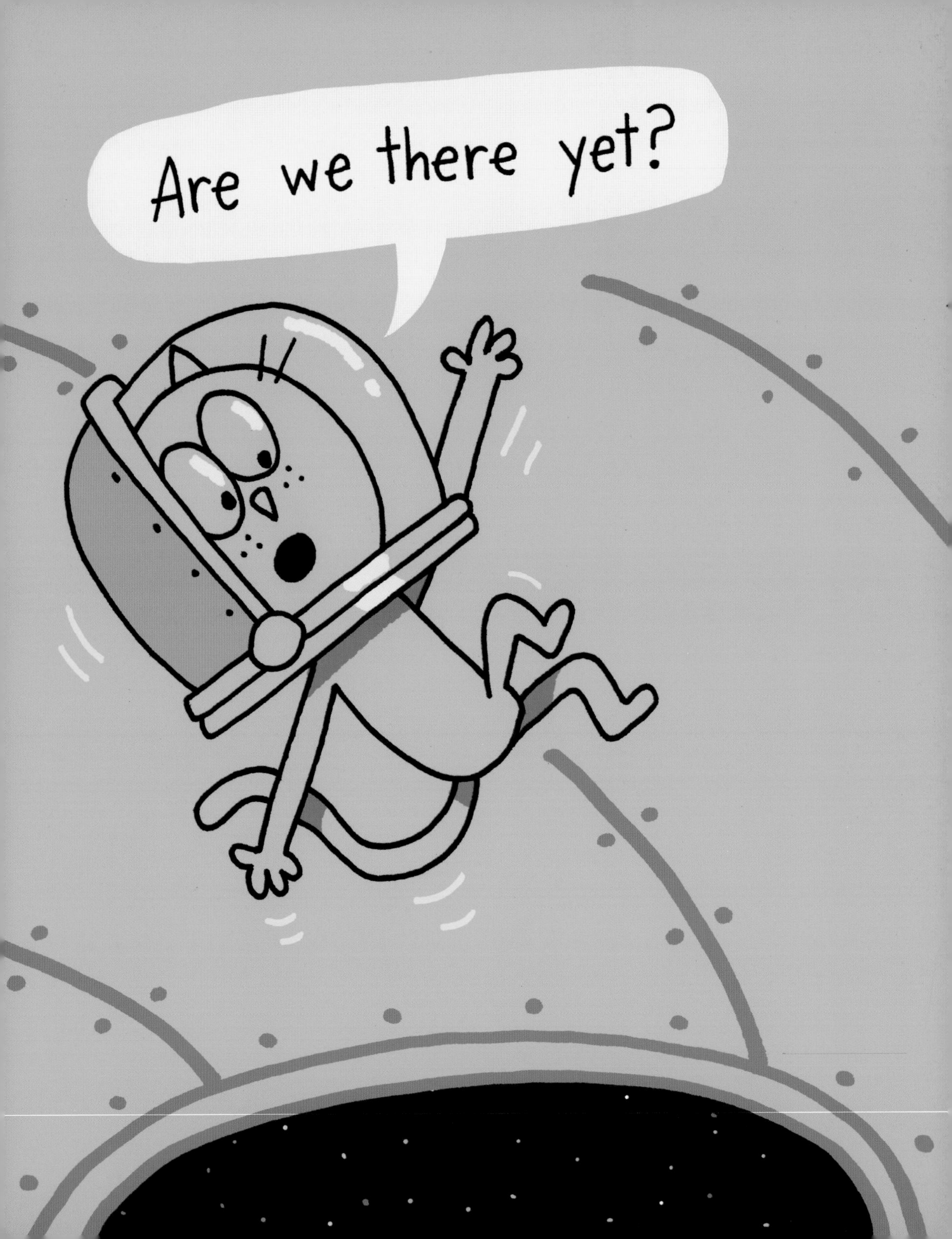
Are we there yet?

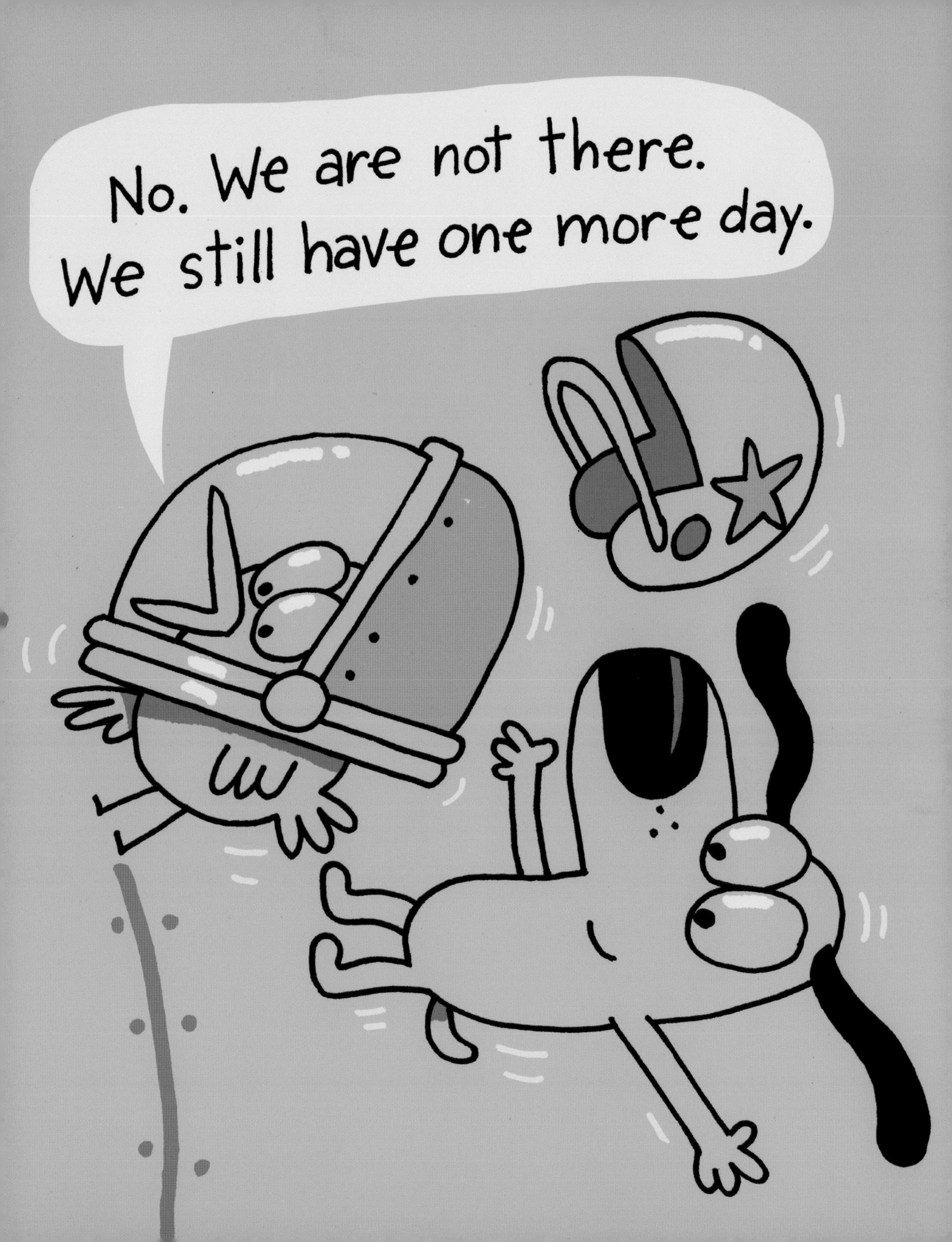
No. We are not there. We still have one more day.

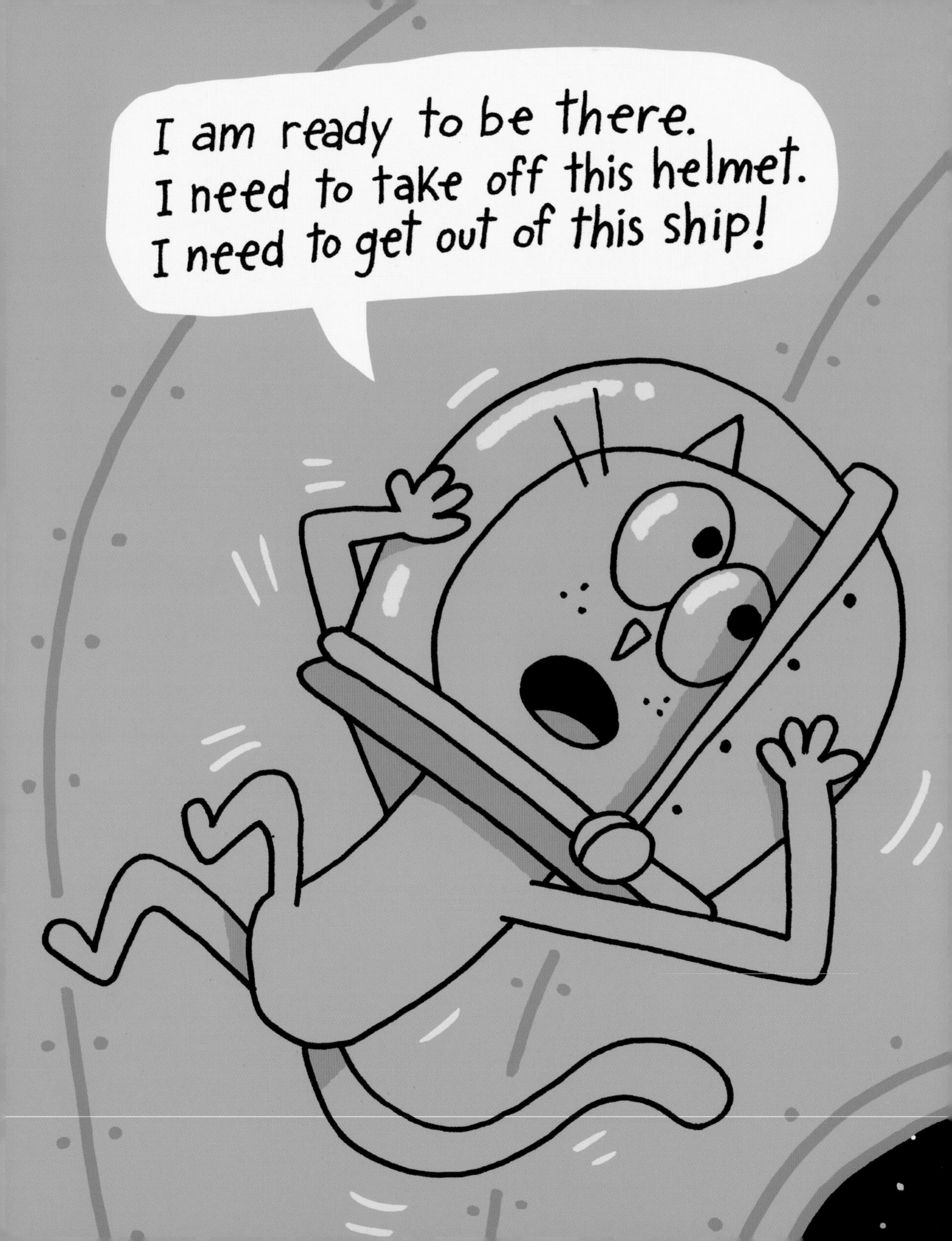
I am ready to be there. I need to take off this helmet. I need to get out of this ship!

I NEED TO GO TO THE BATHROOM!
Don't be funny! There are no bathrooms on the moon!

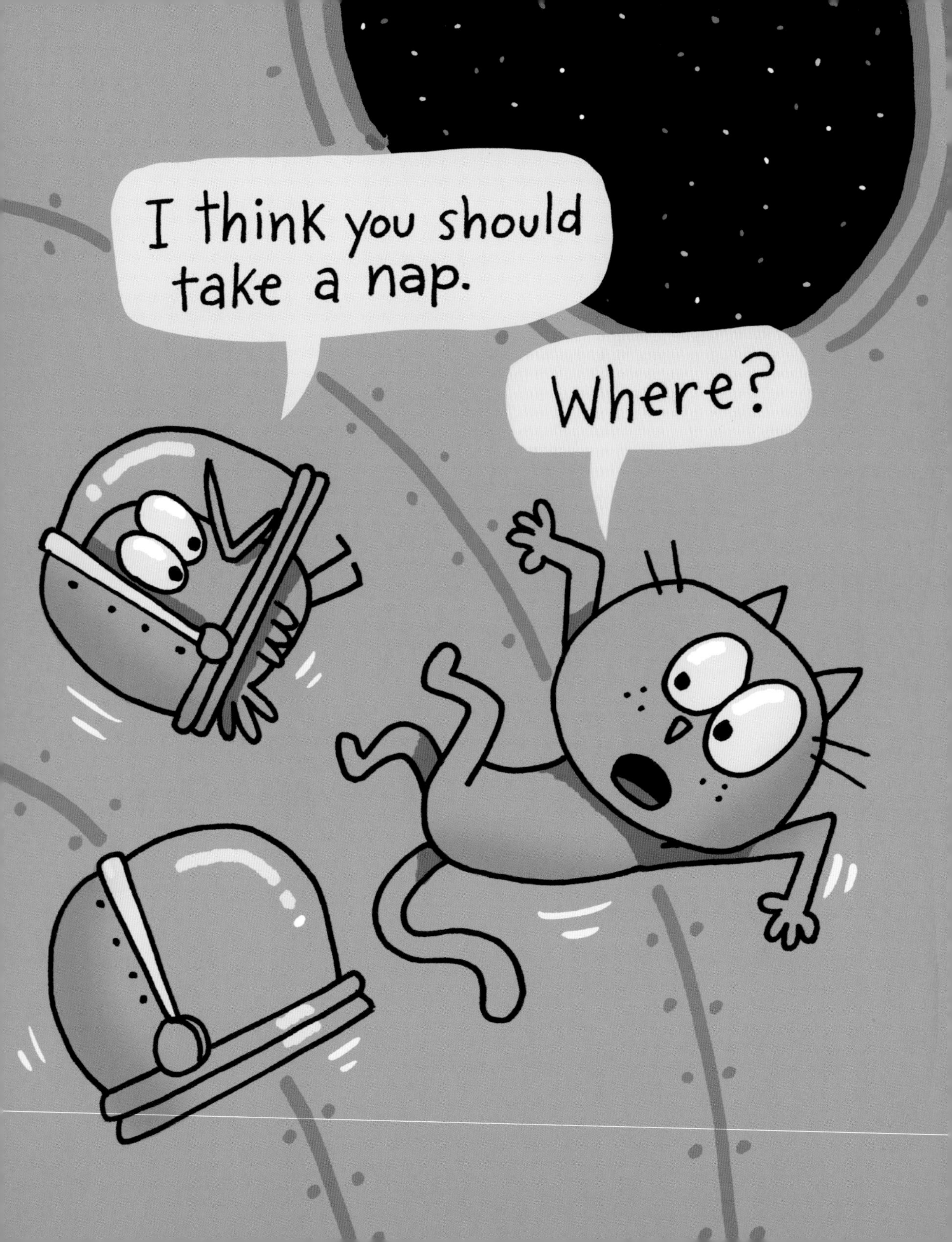
I think you should take a nap.
Where?

In the sleep station. Just float back there, climb into a sleeping bag, and tie the bag to the wall.
I'll try it!

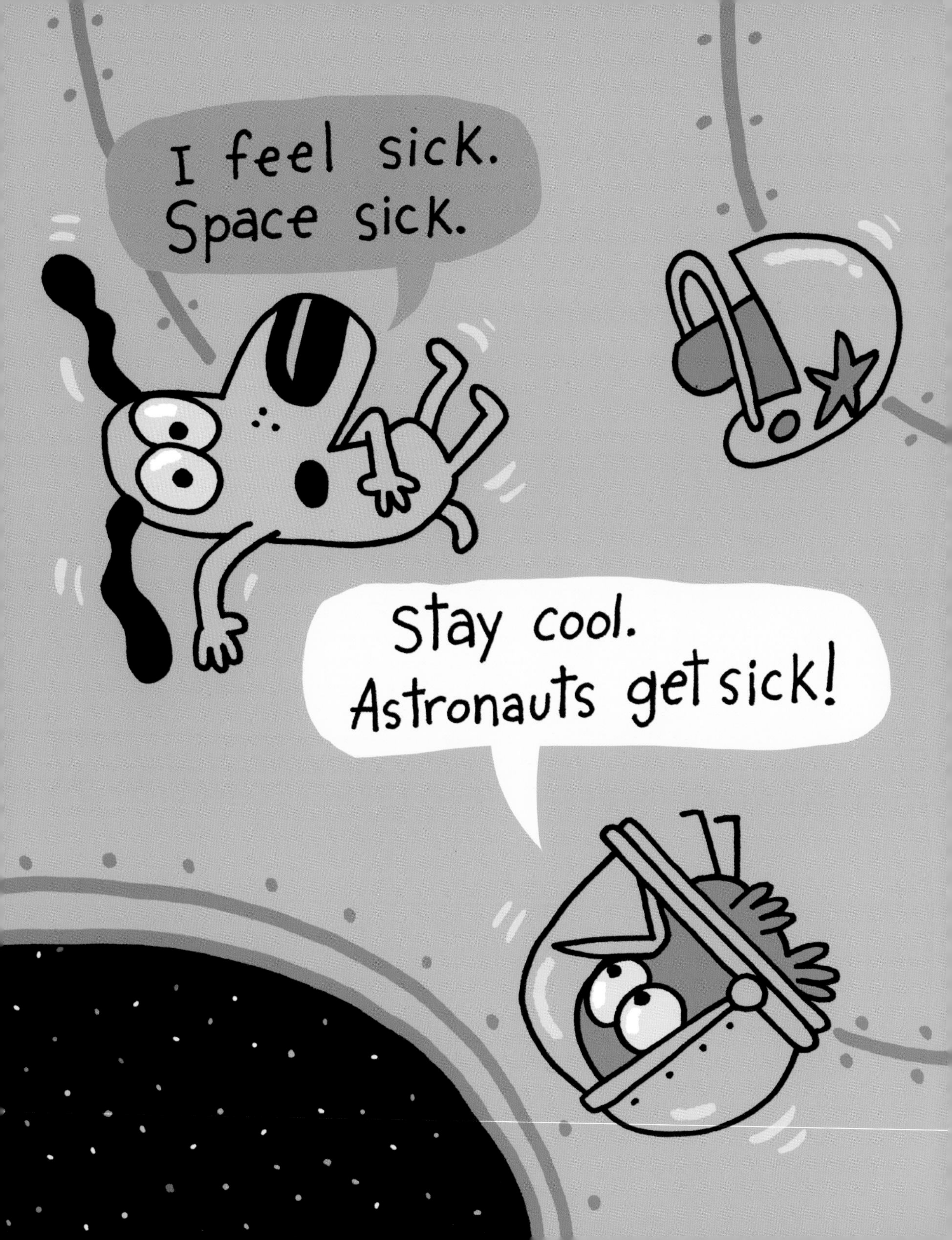
I feel sick. Space sick.
Stay cool. Astronauts get sick!

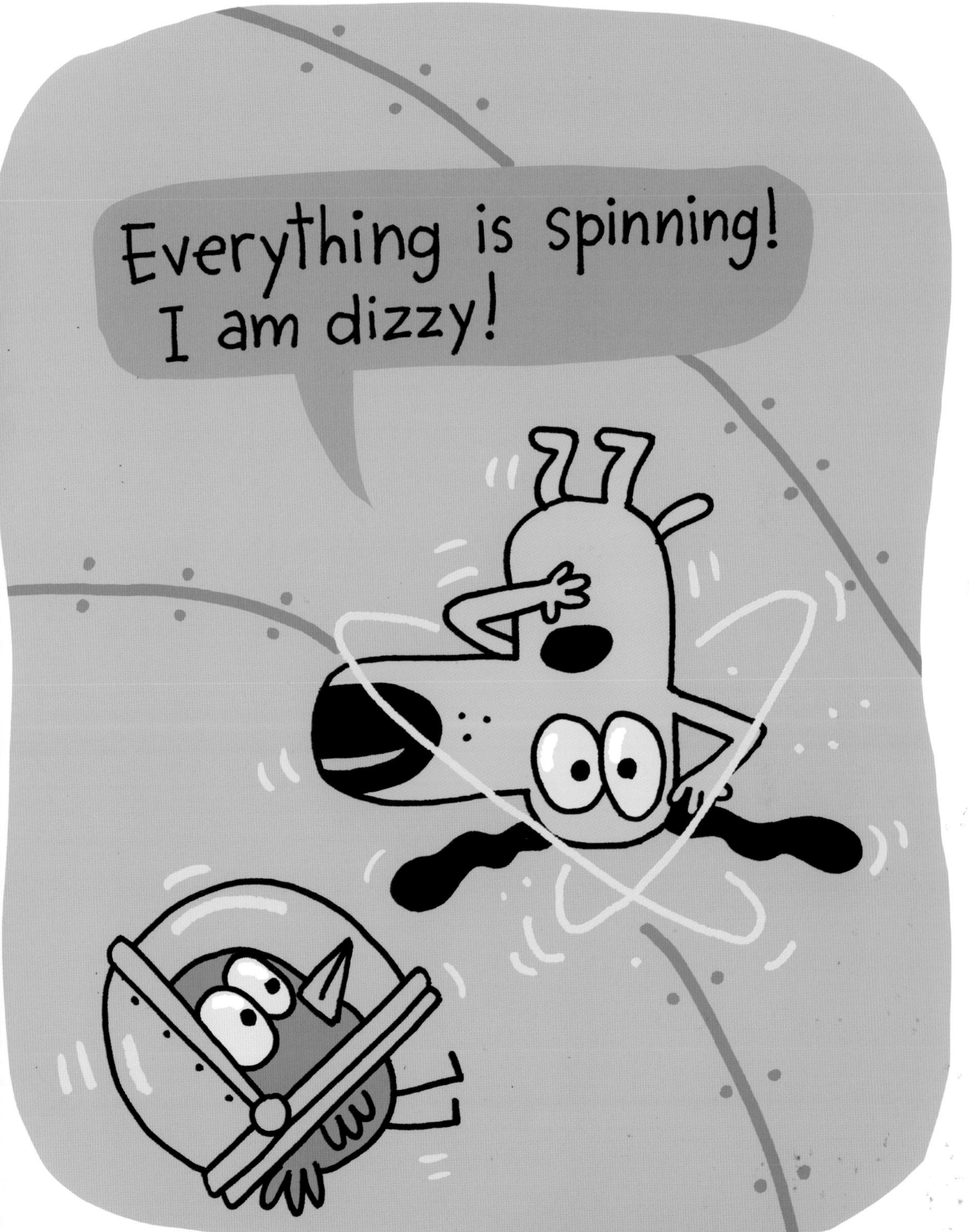
Everything is spinning! I am dizzy!

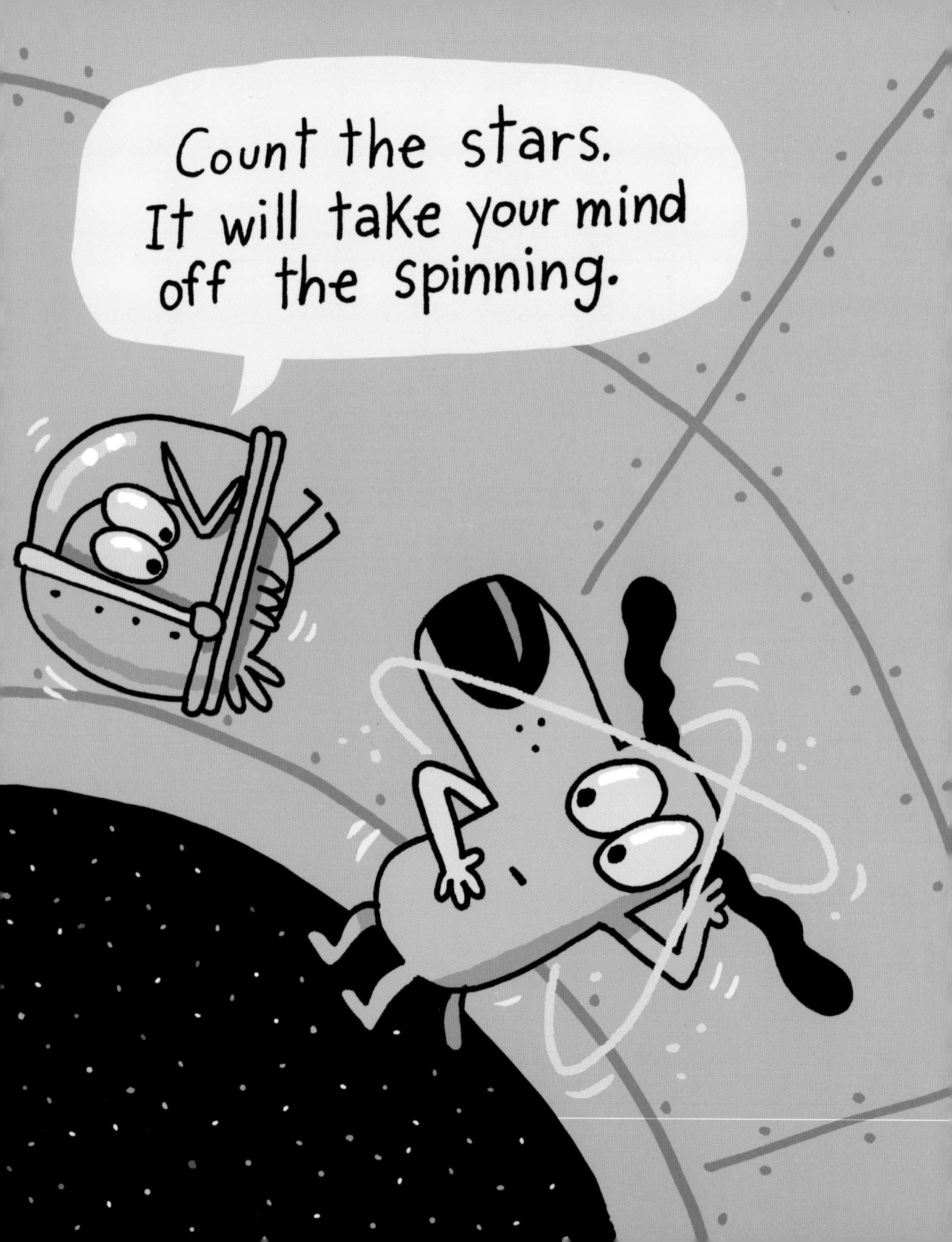
Count the stars. It will take your mind off the spinning.

Are we there yet?
No.
But we are in
the moon's orbit.
We are slowing down.

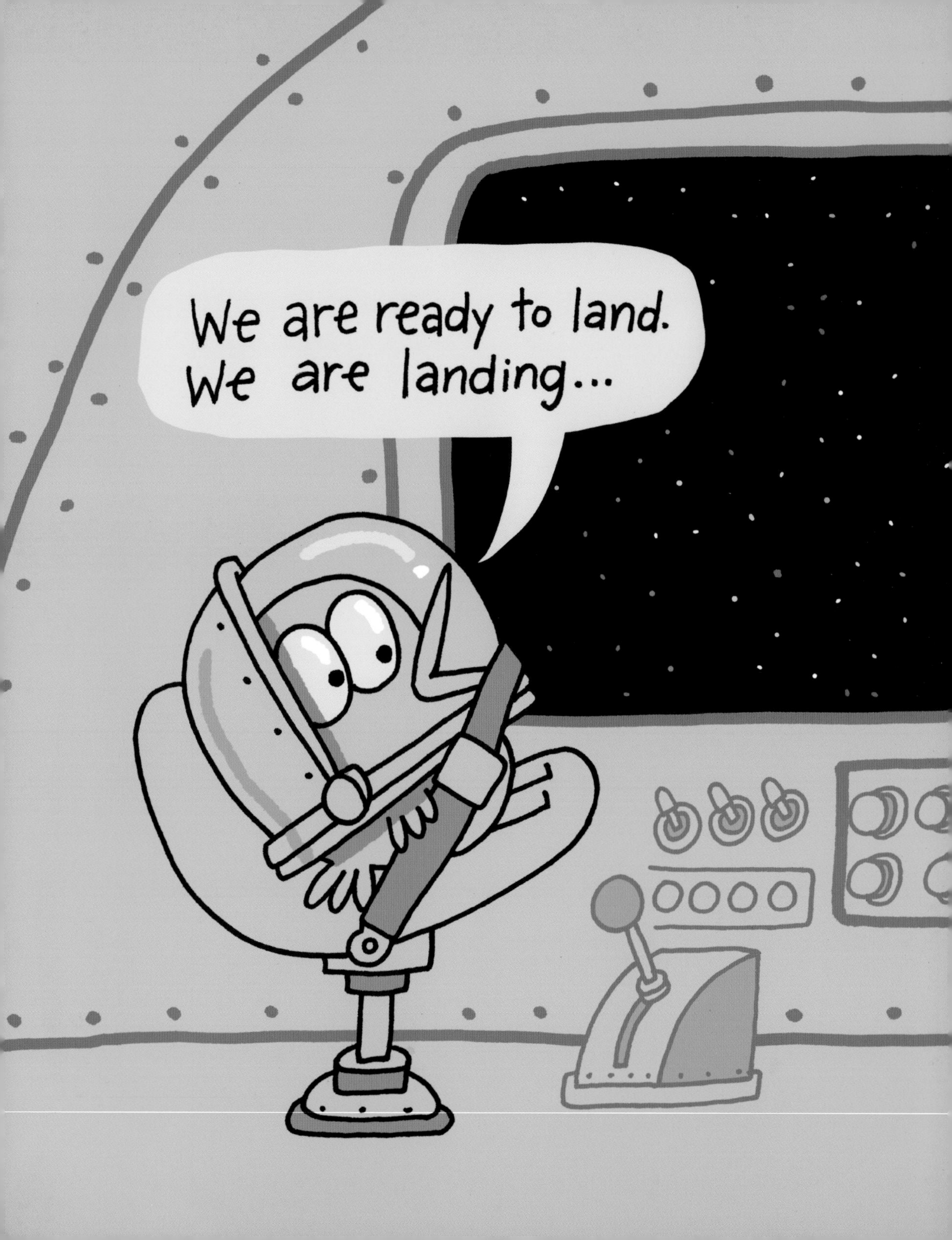
We are ready to land.
We are landing...

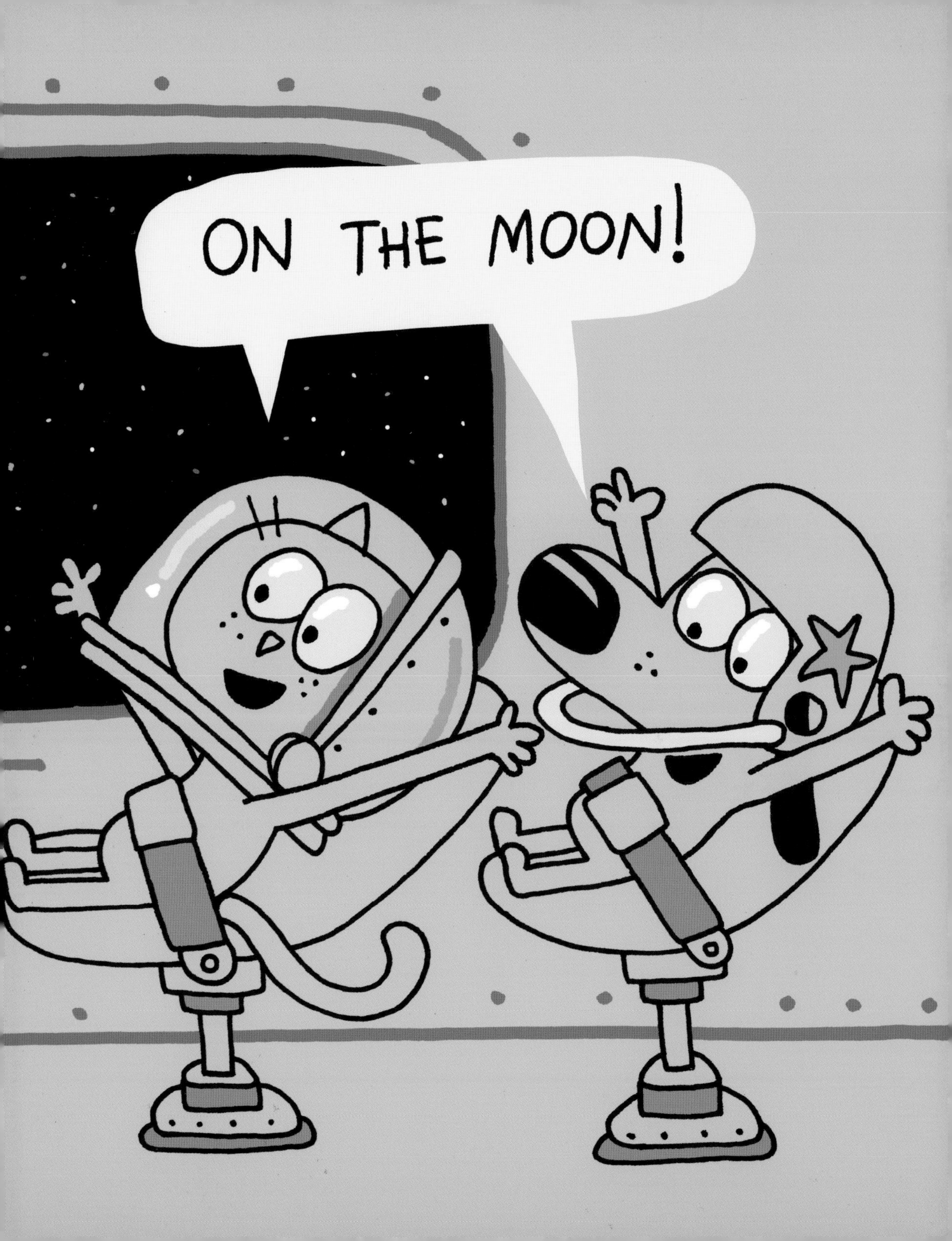
ON THE MOON!

It's one small step for Pup.
And one giant leap for Cat!
And...
A wish come true for Really Bird!

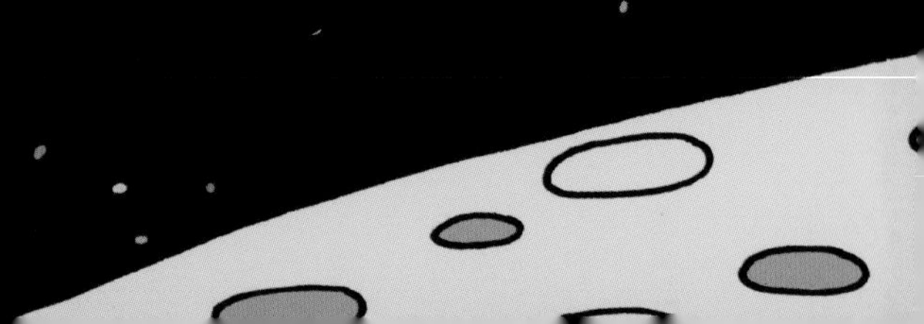

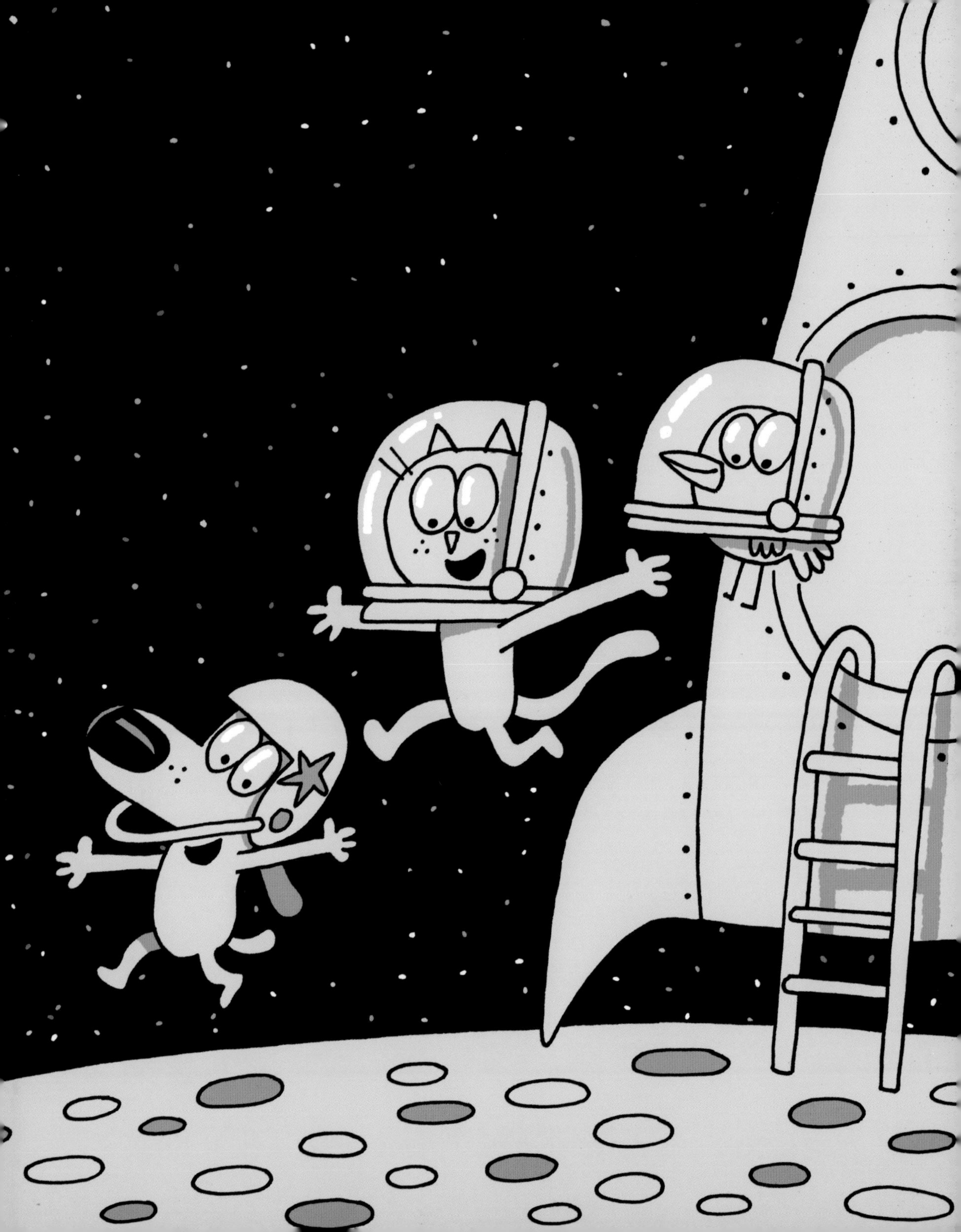

Think About / Talk About:

Really Bird and friends take a "pretend" trip to the moon.

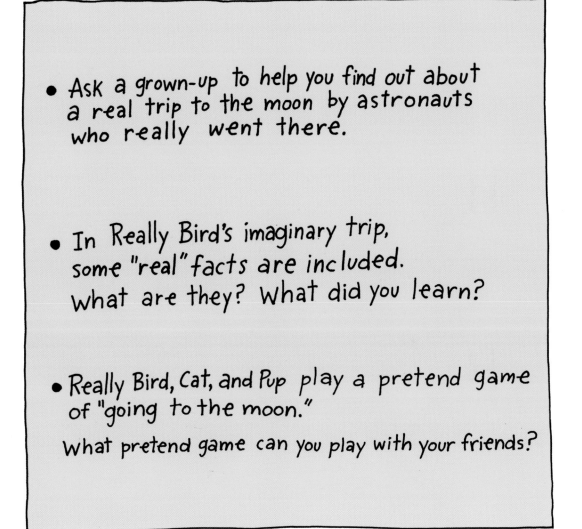

- Ask a grown-up to help you find out about a real trip to the moon by astronauts who really went there.

- In Really Bird's imaginary trip, some "real" facts are included. What are they? What did you learn?

- Really Bird, Cat, and Pup play a pretend game of "going to the moon."

What pretend game can you play with your friends?

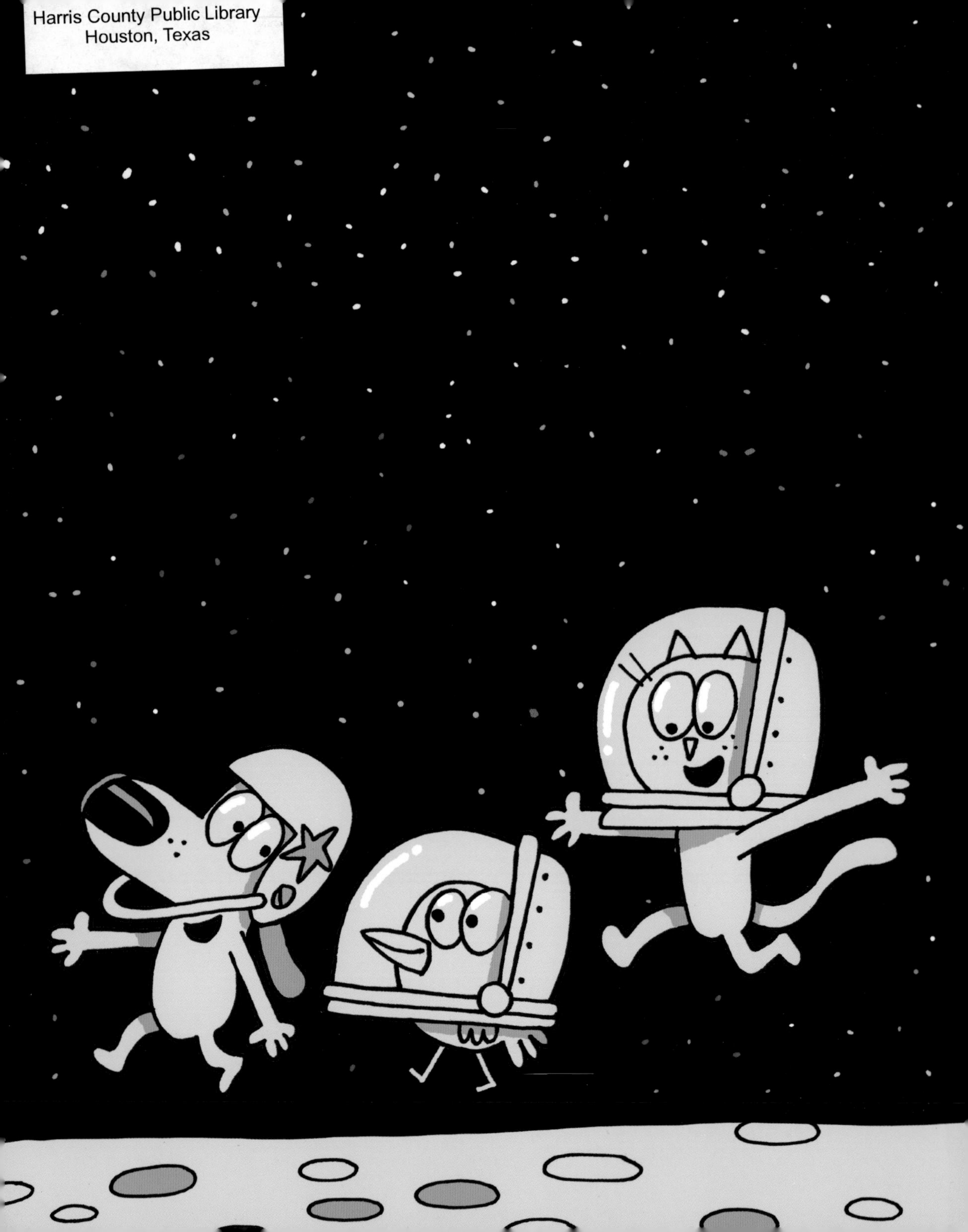